D1036003

CHRISTMAS FOREVER

(THE INN AT SUNSET HARBOR—BOOK 8)

SOPHIE LOVE

ISBN: 978-1-64029-249-9

CHAPTER ONE

Doctor Arkwright smiled at Emily and removed the measuring tape from around her belly. "I can confirm your due date will be December 13th," she said. "You're 37 weeks now, and officially full term."

Emily looked at Daniel and grinned. It was so exciting to know that in just three weeks Baby Charlotte would be joining them.

They all sat back down in their seats, and Doctor Arkwright continued.

"No more flying," she told Emily. "So if you were planning a babymoon, I'm afraid you won't be able to do so abroad."

"Babymoon?" Emily laughed. "I've never even heard of that."

The Doctor chuckled back. "It's all the rage these days. I have mom's and dad's to be planning lavish babymoon's because they know it's their last chance."

Emily found the idea amusing. With everything going on at the inn, it was very unlikely they'd even be able to find the time (not to mention the money) should they even want to go on vacation!

The Doctor clapped her hands. "We're all done here."

"Great," Emily said, hopping down from the seat. "Oh, I almost forgot. I have something for you." She reached in her purse and pulled out Roman's latest album. He'd been delighted to sign it for the Doctor, though thoroughly amused at that same time.

Doctor Arkwright saw what Emily was holding and turned a shade of crimson. She took it hurriedly. "Thanks so much," she whispered.

Emily and Daniel left her surgery and headed out to the parking lot. For the Monday after Thanksgiving, the weather was remarkably warm.

"What are the chances of us missing snow this year?" Emily asked Daniel as she reached the pickup truck.

"Honestly, I can't imagine a Christmas without it," he said. "I'm sure the weather will turn soon enough."

They both got into the truck.

"It's been kinda useful," Emily added. "Think how much more work we've been able to get done at the island thanks to the weather!"

1

Daniel turned his key in the ignition and the old truck juddered to life. "I know," he said, as he began reversing out of his parking space. "We're ahead of schedule. And considering we need everything done by April, that is a very good thing."

Emily thought about how the island had already been booked up, months in advance, before even the roof was on the cabins!

"How are Stu, Clyde and Evan getting along?" she asked him.

"Absolutely fine," he told her. "I didn't know they had it in them. I always thought they were lazy."

Emily laughed but kept her own thoughts about Daniel's friends to herself. She'd grown fond of them over the weeks they'd been working for board and food but that initial impression of them was going to be hard to shake!

"Well I'm glad they're working hard," she told Daniel. "We desperately need the income from the island if things carry on the way they're going."

Daniel glanced across to her in the passenger seat. "Is it really that bad?"

Emily grimaced. "Yes. Unfortunately. We've not had any reservations come in for the winter. In fact, there's no one coming until March. Not in the carriage house, Trevor's house, or the main inn. I've had to cut everyone's shifts as well. It's just Lois and Parker doing some select shifts. Vanessa and Marnie have agreed to take the whole winter off but Matthew's not thrilled by the cut backs. He's trying to save up for a new car. I feel awful. Luckily the restaurant's still getting a lot of bookings so Harry's giving him some work there. The spa's still popular so between the tw of them, they should tide us over. But it's going to be a tight few months."

The timing was either a blessing or a curse. A blessing because it would give Emily the time to spend with her newborn, but a curse because newborns were expensive and the last thing she wanted to be doing was worrying about money!

"It won't," Daniel told her with determination. "I'll get my woodshop up and running before the new year if I have to. You and Baby Charlotte will get everything you need. I promise you."

Emily smiled, and rubbed her round stomach. Daniel was so focused on providing them with the best life possible. It made her so happy. She was so lucky to have him in her life. She just hoped he didn't burn himself out working too hard. It was always a balancing act with Daniel, and he often came down on the wrong side!

"Maybe we should try to get Amy to have her wedding at the inn, like she was planning on with Fraser?" Emily suggested.

2

Daniel barked out his laughter, as if he'd never heard anything so ludicrous. "I highly doubt she'll want to after last time. It would surely bring up some unpleasant memories? And why would Harry want to get married in the place he worked?" He shook his head, thoroughly amused. "It's a shame though. Maybe you can convince another one of your rich friends to get married this year. What about Jane?"

"Absolutely not!" Emily replied. "Jane is *not* the marrying type."

But his suggestion did get her thinking. As they settled into a comfortable silence, Emily tried to imagine some more creative ways to market the inn over the winter. They'd put so much focus on the island, spa, restaurant and speakeasy that they'd neglected to advertize the inn and everything it had to offer properly. Winter weddings could be a good approach, especially with the ballroom for ceremonies and every bedroom in the inn spare for the guests! She'd have to book in a meeting with Bryony, their web-whizz and marketing-extraordinaire.

Daniel turned off the high street then, heading down the smaller road in the direction of Chantelle's school. Their appointment with the doctor had overrun and there wasn't time now to go home first before picking her up.

"Have you heard anymore from Raven Kingsley?" he asked as he drove. "When's the next town meeting to decide on whether her inn can go ahead?"

"I don't know yet," Emily said. "I'm waiting to hear. They'll post a bulletin once the zoning board's had its meeting. I'm sure it won't be for a while yet."

"Aren't you worried?" Daniel asked.

"Of course. Competition, especially from someone like Raven, is always a scary prospect. We've had it easy so far. The market was ours."

"*That* was easy?" Daniel joked, referring to the years and months of work they'd put into making the inn a success.

"You know what I mean," Emily said. "We never really had to worry about bankruptcy before."

"And we do now?" Daniel asked, his jokey expression from before having entirely disappeared.

Emily bit her lip. "Maybe a little," she told him. "If things don't pick up soon. But don't worry, I'll come up with something. A Christmas ball. With Roman singing. For a hundred dollars a ticket!"

She was only joking. Using Roman's celebrity status for her own gain was not something she would ever do. But a Christmas ball for the town might be a nice idea.

Daniel still looked concerned.

"Hun," Emily told him, firmly. "I've got this. Don't worry. Nothing, not even Raven Kingsley's new inn, will stop us. I promise. We're too determined to fail now."

She spoke confidently, but there was also doubt in the back of her mind. What if this was the winter they couldn't weather? What if her perfect life was about to come crashing down around her?

*

Daniel pulled into the school lot. The day was already out and all the kids were playing in the large playground, supervised by their teachers. Emily caught sight of Chantelle, playing with Bailey and Laverne. It was such a relief the girls were friends again.

She got out the pickup truck and waved at Chantelle's teacher on the steps outside the school. She also waved at Tilly, the school's receptionist Emily had recently bonded with. Tilly was having her afternoon coffee break out on the steps with the rest of the faculty. She waved warmly at Emily.

Chantelle must have noticed her parents because she came running over.

"Guess what!" she cried. "We're doing *A Seussified Christmas Carol* for our concert this year!

"What is that?" Emily asked.

"It's Charles Dicken's *A Christmas Carol* but all in rhymes like Doctor Seuss," Chantelle told her. "And I'm playing The Ghost of Christmas Past!"

Emily knew enough to know that was one of the central parts to the play. After Ebenezer Scrooge, the ghost would surely have the most lines.

"Well done sweetheart!" she said, hugging Chantelle tightly.

Once she'd released her, Daniel swept her up into the air.

"What a cool part!" he exclaimed. "I'm so proud of you!"

He placed her back on her feet, and Chantelle reached for something from her satchel.

"These are my lines," she said, holding up a thick booklet with a recognizable Seuss-style illustration on the front of it. "The play will be on Friday 18th December."

4

Emily looked at Daniel, her eyebrows raised. Baby Charlotte would be born by then! Suddenly it all felt incredibly real. And so, so exciting.

"That's not very long to learn all your lines," Daniel said to Chantelle. "Three weeks?"

"I know," she told him, looking suddenly very serious. "But I can do it."

"Of course you can," Emily told her.

They all climbed into the truck and Daniel turned the ignition. It juddered to life with a spluttering noise.

"When I get home, can I start decorating the inn for Christmas?" Chantelle asked from the back seat.

Emily laughed and glanced over her shoulder at her. "We've only just had Thanksgiving."

"I know," Chantelle replied. "But I love Christmas so much. I just can't wait to swap my fall leaves bunting for snowflake bunting."

Daniel started to chuckle. His gaze flicked up to Chantelle in the rear view mirror.

"You can decorate the inn however you want," he said.

Emily smiled to herself. She loved Chantelle's creativity, and she loved the way her home was transformed for every festivity, every season, by the child's hand. She wouldn't swap it for the world -- not the plastic spiders she kept finding down the back of furniture from Halloween or the tiny American flags between the floorboards from July 4th. Her life was perfect. Fingers crossed, it would stay that way.

*

A few minutes later they returned home, and Daniel parked up outside the inn. The vast drive was completely empty now. With no guest cars filling the outside space, the drive looked suddenly enormous.

They went up the porch steps and in through the large door of the inn. As they stepped inside, Emily discovered, to her surprise, that the fall decorations were already gone. She'd only been out the house for a couple of hours, but someone had turned the inn back into a blank canvas. Who could have done so?

She thought of Lois and Marnie using some of their extra time during their slow shift to tidy up, or maybe Vanessa had done it during her cleaning. But then she heard voices coming from the living room and instantly realized who had instigated the tidy up.

5

She went into the living room, and there sat the culprit: Amy. Amy was so organized it was no surprise she'd immediately put their thanksgiving decorations away.

She wasn't alone though. Sat on the couch beside her, by the lit fireplace, with Mogsy's head resting in her lap, drinking what looked like cocoa with marshmallows in, was Patricia. Not only had Emily's mom gotten a taste for marshmallows ever since her first experience of smores, she'd learned to appreciate the love of a smelly, moulting dog. And, more importantly, she'd stayed for the whole thanksgiving weekend. It was a miracle, as far as Emily was concerned, that she and her mom had spent three whole days together without killing one another. Things really did seem to be changing for the better. In fact, Emily was a little melancholy that her mom would be leaving today.

"Amy!" Chantelle cried when she saw Emily's friend sat on the couch. "We're allowed to decorate the inn for Christmas. Did you get the stuff?"

Emily frowned and looked at Daniel, perplexed. By his expression she could tell he was just as curiously amused as she was.

"Of course I did," Amy replied with a grin.

She grabbed a large carrier bag from down the side of the couch, where it had been out of view. Emily could see sparkly silver fabric, glittery snowflakes, and plastic icicles poking out the top of the overstuffed bag.

"What's all that?" she exclaimed. "You've been scheming! The two of you!"

She tickled Chantelle in the ribs and the little girl squealed. Then she wriggled away from Emily's fingers and hurried over to Amy. She grabbed the bag and peered inside.

"This is so cool," she told Amy. "Can we start now?"

Amy looked at Emily as if for approval.

"Don't look at me," Emily laughed, holding her hands up into truce position. "You two have clearly got plans!"

They both scurried into the corridor and began to string fairy lights across the ceiling and spray fake snow on the window panes. Emily watched them from the doorway, her shoulder resting against it. She felt a very strong sense of Christmas cheer.

"My back's killing me," Daniel said then, appearing behind her. "I'm going to take a nice long soak."

"Good idea," she said. "You rest up."

Daniel was working so hard at the moment, trying to provide for the family. She didn't want him getting an injury like his boss

Jack had done recently. That would be a disaster. He needed to take care of himself.

He kissed her cheek, then went upstairs, passing Amy and Chantelle on the way.

"Come on, mommy!" Chantelle cried. "You have to help too!"

Emily had started to feel very tired at this late stage of her pregnancy. But she didn't want to let Chantelle down. She looked over at Patricia, who was flicking through a design magazine whilst sipping her chocolate drink.

"Mom? Want to help too?"

Patricia looked surprised. "Oh. Well. I suppose I could."

Emily smirked, quietly very pleased that her mom would join in. She turned back to Chantelle.

"We're coming!"

Then she and Patricia went out into the hallway and searched through Amy's bag of tricks. Emily took out some glittering tinsel and began winding it around the bannister of the staircase, whilst Patricia selected some sparkly material draped it artistically around the picture frames. It was such a wonderful moment for Emily, so full of peace and happiness.

"When are you getting married, Amy?" Chantelle asked as she affixed snowflakes to the walls with sticky tack.

"I haven't set the date yet," Amy told her, smiling to herself. "I can't work out what season I want my wedding to be in. Or even what country."

Chantelle's eyes widened as though the thought of an overseas wedding had never even crossed her mind. "You could get married in Lapland! Reindeers and white snow!"

Amy laughed. "I was thinking more the Bahamas. Turtles... and white beach."

"That sounds nice too," Chantelle conceded.

"If you need any help planning it," Emily said. "I'd be very happy to help. You were so great with my wedding, I'd love to return the favor."

Amy looked touched. "Really, Em? That would be the best. But honestly, you're the one who's got a ton of stuff to organize before I'm even ready to get married. You've got to give birth, for starters! And what about a babymoon? You're running out of time."

Emily laughed and shook her head. "Not you too! A babymoon? My doctor asked us if we were going on one. Is this a new thing?"

"What's a babymoon?" Chantelle chimed in.

disturbing any of the guests. And somewhere to keep their toys so they don't end up all over the place."

Emily was so touched. The room was lovely. It just needed to be filled with toys now!

"I love it, thank you so much guys," she said, hugging Amy and Chantelle in turn.

They went back into the living room so Emily could have a rest before the rest of the decorating commenced. Then, once she felt rejuvenated, they took on the mammoth task of decorating the ballroom.

"You know there's something missing," Emily said, once she'd strung up the last of the fairy lights.

"What's that?" Chantelle asked.

"A Christmas tree!" Emily cried.

Chantelle's eyes grew round and excited. "Of course. But we need more than one, don't we? We need one for the ballroom and one for the hallway. And one for Trevor's. And the spa. And the restaurant."

"Sounds like you need a whole forest," Amy joked.

"How about we all go tomorrow?" Emily suggested. "Yvonne was telling me about an amazing Christmas Tree farm out of town. It's not the one we went to last year, it's supposed to be really huge. We could make a day of it?"

"Can Nana Patty come too?" Chantelle asked.

Emily shook her head. "She's leaving today," she said.

Chantelle's expression became downcast. Emily hated to see her sad.

"Why don't you ask her?" she suggested.

Patricia had been surprising her recently. Maybe she'd stick around if they made it clear they wanted her too.

Chantelle bounded out the ballroom and down the corridor, to where Patricia was relaxing in the living room.

"Nana Patty!" Chantelle cried, her voice loud enough to carry all the way to where Emily was waddling through the house, trying to catch up to her. "Can you come Christmas tree shopping with us tomorrow?"

Emily entered the living room, just as Patricia was shaking her head.

"I have a flight booked to get me home," Patricia said. "It's leaving this evening."

"Please," Chantelle said. She got onto the couch beside Patricia and wrapped her arms around her neck. "I really, really want you to stay."

Patricia looked stunned by the affection. She patted Chantelle's arm and looked up at Emily standing in the doorway. Emily smiled, touched by the sweet scene, by how much love Chantelle had to give, even to those who had behaved in ways that ought to preclude it. Her capacity for forgiveness and kindness always inspired Emily.

"Well, I don't want to be in the way," Patricia said, speaking to Chantelle but directing her words at Emily.

"You're not in the way," Emily said. "We've loved having you here. And it's not like the inn is busy at the moment. It's the perfect time to stay. If you want."

"Please!" Chantelle begged.

Finally, Patricia smiled. "Okay. I will stay and help you pick out a tree."

Emily could tell that Patricia was touched to be invited, to be welcome in after all her bad behavior and the terrible fights they'd had. Emily felt an overwhelming sense of gratitude then, realizing that life could always change for the better. It seemed that one was never too old to feel Christmas cheer for the first time!

CHAPTER TWO

Chantelle looked overjoyed when Emily and Daniel arrived to pick her up from school the next day, with Patricia sitting patiently in the back seat. She looked very out of place in the truck in her two-piece outfit and blazer combo but Chantelle didn't seem to notice. She leaped into the backseat, beaming, her cheeks pink from the chilly weather.

"Christmas tree time!" she declared.

Daniel drove them. The weather still hadn't fully turned yet, though it was much colder than it had been. There wasn't even any frost, which was common at this time of year. Emily was grateful that the weather had held up so far. It meant that Evan, Clyde and Stu had been able to do their work on the island unimpeded.

The Christmas Tree farm was quite a way out of Sunset Harbor. They could, of course, just go to the depot at Ellsworth, but that was hardly a magical experience for Chantelle! So they went even further, to the one in Taunton Bay.

As they pulled down the small, bumpy, potholed road that lead to the farm, Emily could see the extra journey was well worth it. The Christmas Tree farm was enormous, and thanks to the sloping hillside that ran all the way down from the road to the lake, they had an amazing view of all the trees.

"It's like a whole forest of Christmas," Chantelle said, in awe.

Daniel pulled up into the makeshift lot, which was really just a patch of flattened ground, covered in hay to stop it becoming too muddy. There was a small wood-panelled house to one side, with a handmade sign proclaiming; Christmas Trees!

Emily looked over at Patricia in the backseat beside Chantelle. She was wearing her typical snooty expression, and peering out the window with a fearful expression for the dirty ground she was about to step on. But she held her tongue and Emily smiled to herself. That, in itself, felt like a small victory.

Everyone climbed out of the pickup truck, just at the same time the front door to the house opened. A man stepped out, waving at them. He seemed very jolly, with a round belly. Emily wondered if he'd ever considered becoming a Santa, he certainly had the look for it.

"Hi folks!" he said, grinning. "I'm Terry. Are you here to cut down your own tree?"

"We certainly are," Daniel said.

Chantelle hurried up to the man. "Actually, we need five trees. We have an inn, you see, and a restaurant and spa and they all need a tree. So does the ballroom."

"How about we just start with one?" Emily suggested, thinking of the fact there were no guests at the inn right now to enjoy the trees. "Then if we need more, we can come back for another day trip."

That seemed to please Chantelle, and she nodded in agreement.

Terry showed them the tools they would need, then they waved goodbye and headed out into the forest of trees. Emily thought of the farm they'd visited last year, which had been very busy, run more like a fare with tractor rides and hot chocolate to purchase. She liked this more back-to-basics experience, especially since the moment they were inside the forest everything became very quiet.

"It's like we're the only people in the world," she said, her hands protectively cradling her bump.

She looked back to see how Patricia was getting on. Despite walking on her tiptoes and wearing a slightly pinched expression, she wasn't complaining at all. Emily wondered if perhaps she might be enjoying herself, though too proud to admit it.

"Nana Patty," Chantelle said, hurrying back and grasping her hand. "I think there's some really, really dark green ones over here. Come on!"

Emily smiled to herself as she watched her daughter pull her mom along. She couldn't recall a time when Patricia had been so compliant, joining in with an activity. Chantelle was clearly rubbing off on her.

Daniel put an arm around Emily's shoulders, bringing her body close to his.

"This is wonderful, isn't it?" he said. "I love how enthusiastic she gets about these sort of things. I can't wait to see how much she enjoys Hanukkah."

"What date does it start this year?" Emily asked him.

"Sixteenth."

"So after Charlotte has joined us?" she asked, grinning, thinking about having a newborn in the house during this wonderful time of the year, when everyone was celebrating.

"Maybe even on the first day," he said, smiling. "Wouldn't that be lovely?"

Emily nodded in agreement. It would certainly be delightful for Daniel to have his daughter born on such a significant day.

Just then, they heard Chantelle calling through the trees.

"Mom! Dad! We've got it!"

They smiled at one another then trudge towards her voice. Chantelle was standing next to gorgeous tree, with the darkest pines Emily had ever seen. It was wonderfully symmetrical, too, the sort of perfect tree that would be used in magazines. And of course, it was enormous.

"Nana Patty chose it," Chantelle said, looking proudly at Patricia.

"Did she now?" Emily asked, pleased to see how well the two were bonding.

Even Patricia looked quietly pleased.

"In that case," Daniel said, "Nana Patty ought to have the first go."

"Oh goodness, no," Patricia said, shaking her hands at the saw Daniel was offering her.

"Yes!" Chantelle cried, jumping up and down, clapping her hands. "Please Nana Patty! It's really fun. I promise you'll enjoy it."

Patricia hesitated, then finally relented. "Oh, all right then. If you insist."

She took the saw from Daniel and glared at the tree like it was an enemy. Daniel bent down and moved the large branches out of her way, exposing the truck where she was to cut. Patricia squatted, clearly in an attempt to not let her knee touch the muddy ground. Emily couldn't help but laugh to herself. Her mom looked like a frog!

Patricia reached in and sawed across the trunk of the tree. She squealed, elated, and looked back at the family watching on.

"You're right," she said to Chantelle. "That *is* fun!"

Emily chuckled aloud. Just a few days in Maine with her family and Patricia had eaten smores and chopped wood!

Terry arrived then with his tractor and put the tree in the back.

"All aboard," he said.

They all got into the back with the tree, but Patricia didn't move. She looked stunned.

"You want me to ride in that?"

Chantelle bounced up and down on the wooden bench. "It's fun! You have to trust me!"

"Do I have a choice?" Patricia asked.

Chantelle shook her head, still grinning wickedly.

Patricia sighed and climbed into the tractor trailer.

Once everyone was settled, Terry drove them back to their car and helped Daniel secure the very large tree onto the roof of his truck. Then they paid him and left the farm, all feeling exhilarated.

"I can't wait to decorate it," Chantelle said. "Will you help Nana Patty?"

Patricia nodded. "Yes, but then I must leave after that. Okay?"

Chantelle pouted, looking a little sad. "If you have too. But I've loved you being here. Will you come back for Christmas?"

Emily watched her mom in the rear-view mirror. She couldn't even recall the last time they'd spent Christmas together. Even when she was living in New York with Ben, they'd tended to spend Christmas with his family rather than Patricia. It wasn't like the woman ever particularly got into the Christmas spirit and it seemed like a dumb idea as far as Emily was concerned to put themselves through the misery. She wondered whether the softer side of Patricia she'd seen over the last few days could extend that far.

"Maybe," she said, evasively. "I think your mother and father might have a lot on at that point in time. The baby will be born by then, won't she?"

"Even better!" Chantelle pressed. "She needs to meet her Nana Patty."

Clearly realizing that she'd come up against Patricia's stubborn side, Chantelle offered another suggestion. "Or if not Christmas, maybe New Years? We have a party at the inn. You can come to that, right?"

Patricia remained evasive in her answers. "We will have to see," was all she'd commit to.

Chantelle looked over at Emily next. "Do you think Papa Roy might want to come for Christmas?" she asked.

Emily felt tense. It was even less likely her father would be able to come with his health deteriorating.

"We can ask," Emily told her, and the conversation died down to silence.

They reached the inn and Daniel parked up. Stu, Clyde and Evan were home, so they came out to help carry the tree inside. Then, together, the four men heaved it up into its position in the foyer.

"That's one big tree," Clyde said, whistling. He wiped the perspiration from his forehead and looked down at Chantelle. "How are you going to get the angel on the top? Even on my shoulders I don't think you'll make it."

To iterate his point, he swept a giggling Chantelle up into his strong arms and plonked her on his shoulders. He began parading her around. Emily noticed Patricia wincing. Probably worrying about the hard wooden floor beneath them, a mother's instinct that even Patricia possessed!

"I'll go get the ladder," Stu said, heading off in the direction of the garage.

Evan and Clyde helped, too, by carrying all the boxes of decorations out of the garage. Then the three men headed off into town to watch the game and have a drink after their long day working on the island, leaving just the family to decorate.

"We need to put on Christmas music," Emily said, heading over to the reception desk where the sound system was set up. She found an old Christmas Crooners CD and put it on. Frank Sinatra's voice filled the hall.

"And," Daniel added. "We need to have hot chocolates!"

Chantelle nodded enthusiastically, and they all hurried into the kitchen. Daniel boiled milk on the stove, while Chantelle searched the pantry for leftover marshmallows. She returned with not only marshmallows, but also rainbow sprinkles and whipped cream.

"Excellent," Daniel said, as he poured them each a mug of hot chocolate, then topped them with cream, marshmallows and sprinkles.

Emily had never seen Patricia consume anything like that in her life! The smores had been a sight enough to behold, but this was a whole other thing. It was like Patricia had been transformed by the spirit of Christmas, at last, after sixty-odd years of resistance!

They headed back into the hall, where the giant Christmas tree stood waiting to be decorated, and got to work. Of course, Chantelle took the lead.

"We need lights over here, Daddy," she said to Daniel, pointing at a bare patch. "And Nana Patty, those reindeer need to be on this branch."

Emily leaned in to her mom and said, "Chantelle has a very specific vision."

Patricia laughed. "Yes, I can tell. She has an eye for detail. She'll make a wonderful interior designer one day."

Emily could certainly picture it. Either that, or some kind of events organizer. She touched her bump, wondering what kind of personality Baby Charlotte would have, whether she'd be similar to her sister -- a leader, organizer, socializer, performer -- or whether she'd have a different way about her. Perhaps she'd take after Emily herself, and be less inclined towards the limelight, more content to read a book and take the dogs on quiet, countryside walks. Or perhaps she'd be like her father, practical and hardworking, prone to moments of broodiness. Or, as Emily tended to think, she might take after the aunt for which she was named; sweet, imaginative, inquisitive, calm. She couldn't wait to find out.

"Nana Patty," Chantelle said then, breaking through Emily's reverie. "What was mommy like when she was my age?"

Patricia was busy stretching a large piece of sparkly tinsel across the branches, weaving it through them so it wouldn't fall.

"At eight-years-old? Well let me think. Her hair was very curly then, much more than it is now. She used to wear these beautiful plaid dresses. Do you remember darling?"

Emily cast her mind back in time. The plaid dress and itchy tights combo her mom always dressed her up in had been a source of numerous fights. Emily had hated the way she wasn't allowed to run or climb trees because Patricia didn't want her to mess up her clothes.

"I remember," she replied.

Patricia continued. "Her father was teaching her piano then as well. She was quite good at it but lost interest."

Emily wished now that she hadn't. That she'd continued to sit beside her dad on that battered piano stool, learning songs from musicals and old classics. Those were precious times and she hadn't made the most of them. She hadn't known that she needed to.

"Papa Roy?" Chantelle asked.

"Yes," Patricia said. She smiled. "He was very gifted at the piano. And he loved it. That's why he had to have one in this house, even though we were only here a few weeks a year. But he'd light the fire and play us the piano, and Emily would wrap herself up in a blanket and fall asleep." She let out a melancholy sigh. "There were always wonderful moments in between, weren't there, sweetheart?"

Emily knew what she meant. In between the pain of losing Charlotte. That after her death, when the silence grew between her parents like an invisible wall of glass, there were some moments of normalcy, of joy, even, when the quietness was filled with beauty and their minds were given a reprieve from grief.

"I love Papa Roy," Chantelle told Patricia. "Was he a very good husband?"

Patricia looked back at Chantelle. And to Emily's shock and surprise, she reached out and stroked the girl's head.

"He was. Not always. But no one is perfect."

"Did you love him?"

"With all my heart."

"What about now?" Chantelle asked.

"Hush," Emily interrupted. "That's a personal question."

"I don't mind," Patricia said. She looked Chantelle squarely then, and spoke in an undeterred voice. "We spent many years as husband and wife, many good years. But we weren't happy and the most important thing in life is to be happy. It was very hard to say goodbye to him, but in the end it was for the best. And yes, I still love him now. Once you love someone you can never really stop."

Emily turned away then, wiping the tear that had formed in the corner of her eye. During her entire lifetime, Patricia had only ever bad-mouthed her father. Never once had she heard her admit that she still loved Roy.

Silence fell then, and the family quietly put the last decorations on the tree. The melancholy air that hovered around them dissipated only when Daniel took the angel statue out of the box.

"It's time," he said, handing it to Chantelle.

With an excited smile on her face, Chantelle climbed the ladder, stretched her arm as long as she could, and placed the angel on the top branch of the tree.

"Ta da!" she cried.

Daniel helped her back down the ladder and everyone stepped back to admire their handywork. Emily felt overcome with emotion as it occurred to her that this was the first tree she had decorated alongside her mom for close to twenty years. Patricia had withdrawn from the ritual shortly after Charlotte's death. But now, with a new family around her, and a new child growing inside Emily, she had come back. The timing felt poignant to Emily, as if the spirit of Charlotte had had a hand in making it happen.

"I think this is the most beautiful tree I've ever seen," she said, looking with gratitude to each of her family members.

*

With the tree complete and the hot chocolates drunk, it was time for Patricia to say goodbye.

"I wish you didn't have to leave," Chantelle said, clasping her arms around Patricia's waist.

Emily watched her mom hug the child back, looking significantly less awkward than she usually did with overt displays of affection.

"We can speak on the telephone, if you want to," Patricia told the child.

"Will you Face Time with us?" Chantelle exclaimed, her face breaking into a huge grin.

"Will I what now?" Patricia asked, looking bemused.

"Video messaging, mom," Emily explained. "Chantelle loves it."

"We video message with Papa Roy all the time," Chantelle told her. "Can we? Can we? Can we?"

Patricia nodded. "Of course. If that's what you want."

She looked genuinely touched, Emily thought, that Chantelle would want to keep in contact with her.

"And," Emily added, "Please do think about coming for Christmas. We would love to have you."

"I don't want to get in the way," Patricia said.

Daniel piped up then. "You wouldn't be in the way," he said. "We have no bookings at the moment. If you want a bit of your own space we could even put you in the carriage house."

"Well," Patricia said, looking like she was trying to hide her touched expression. "I will certainly consider it."

Her cab arrived then, coming down the long drive, its tires crunching on the gravel. Daniel picked up Patricia's case and carried it down the porch steps. The rest of the family followed. Even Mogsy and Rain came out to see her off, wagging their tails in unison as they peered through the posts.

Daniel put the case in the trunk, then hugged Patricia goodbye. Chantelle clung to her.

"I love you Nana Patty," she exclaimed. "Please come back soon."

"I will darling," Patricia said, stroking her head. "It won't be long at all."

Then it was Emily's turn. She hugged her mother, feeling herself filled with gratitude and appreciation. It may have taken years to get to this point -- and the horrible, sobering shock of Roy's illness -- but it seemed like things were finally changing for the better between them.

"Please stay in touch," Emily said to her mom.

"I will," Patricia replied. "I promise."

They released one another and Patricia climbed into the cab. Emily joined her family, feeling Daniel's arm reach around her shoulders and Chantelle's hands clinging onto her. She cradled her bump with one hand, and waved goodbye to her mom with the other. They stayed there until the cab had disappeared out of sight.

As they turned back to head into the inn, Emily heard the phone start to ring. She went over to the reception desk and answered it. It was Amy's voice on the other end.

"Em, I just saw the bulletin outside the town hall," she said.

Emily was still struggling to wrap her head around the fact that Amy was a Sunset Harbor resident, that she paid attention to the goings on of their little town.

"What bulletin?" Emily asked.

"Raven's inn! The meeting is tomorrow. The one they postponed until after Thanksgiving."

"Tomorrow?" Emily exclaimed. "That's a bit short notice! And hardly much of a postponement!"

"I know. What do you think it means that it's so soon?"

"I can only assume that means the zoning board came to a quick and unanimous decision," Emily told her, recalling the process of getting her own inn licence.

"A unanimous yes or a unanimous no?"

"We'll find out soon enough."

Amy sounded incredibly stressed about the whole thing, which Emily found a little odd considering she was the one who'd be most affected by the outcome.

"We have to go to the meeting," she said brusquely. "Can you clear your calendar?"

"Maybe. I'm not sure why I need to though. I already said my piece."

She could hear the impatience in Amy's voice. "Emily, you have to go. You have to shoot it down! If Raven opens an inn in Sunset Harbor your business will struggle."

"You should have more faith in me," Emily told her. "I don't mind competition."

"Well you should," Amy told her. "Especially coming from Raven Kingsley. She'll crush you."

Emily thought of the moments she'd spent with Raven. They hadn't bonded, as such, but they were on friendly terms. Raven had helped her when Daniel was in his boating accident, and she'd even come to the town Thanksgiving dinner Emily had thrown. She perceived Raven's inn as friendly competition.

"What makes you say that?" Emily said, shaking her head. "Raven's just like any other business owner. She wants to work hard and make a success of herself. I know she's been a bit of a vulture in the past, but she wants to settle here. Her husband left her and she just wants the kids to be in one place for some stability."

"I think you're being naive," Amy said. "A leopard doesn't change its spots."

"Amy, my mother just drank hot chocolate with cream and marshmallows and chopped and helped saw down a Christmas tree. Leopards, like dragons, can, indeed, change their spots."

But Amy wasn't backing down. "Raven will drive you out of business then head to the next town. It's what she does. She's got a history of doing it, destroying local areas with her big, flashy hotels. It's all corporate, soulless. The last thing the town needs. And she has so many of them, she makes the room prices dirt cheap to start with. Even if she runs a loss for the first five years she'll do it, just so she can eliminate the competition!"

Emily couldn't reconcile the Raven Amy was talking about and the one she'd become acquaintances with. But hearing what Amy had to say was starting to rattle her.

"Just come to the meeting," Amy said.

"Okay," Emily said.

As she placed the receiver down, she wondered whether Amy was right. Maybe Raven was as ruthless as all that. But if Emily didn't have the inn, what would become of her? Of her family? Suddenly, she felt as if the ground beneath her was becoming unstable. What if the dream life she was living turned out to be temporary after all...?

CHAPTER THREE

The next day after dropping Chantelle at school, Daniel drove Emily to Harry and Amy's house before heading off to work. When Emily rang the doorbell, Amy answered, beaming from ear to ear.

"Ready?" Emily asked.

Amy's grin only widened. "You bet!"

Today Amy was having a bonanza shopping day, with appointments booked at potential wedding venues and several house viewings with real estate agents. And since Harry was working in the restaurant all day, Emily was on hand to offer support and words of wisdom. She was, of course, thrilled to be helping.

They got into Amy's white Chrysler and set off.

"Where's the first viewing?" Emily asked from the passenger seat.

"Eastern Road," Amy said, as she looked over her steering wheel for traffic. Seeing none, she turned onto the main street.

"Ooh," Emily said. "That's a nice part of town. The other side of the harbor to me, but still close."

"Especially in comparison to New York," Amy joked. "There's a brochure in the glove compartment. Take a look."

Emily reached inside and, finding the glossy folder, opened it up. She browsed through the slips of paper inside. Amongst the legal information and property details -- three bedrooms, Emily noted with a knowing smile -- she found a selection of photographs. The house looked gorgeous. If Harry and Amy were indeed planning to start their own family soon, this would be the place to do it! She smiled to herself, but then caught sight of the eye-wateringly huge asking price and almost choked.

"That one has an outside studio space," Amy informed Emily as she drove. "They're using it as an art studio at the moment but I'd turn it into an office. If I'm going to be working from home full time I'd like to have a separate space, you know?"

"Sure," Emily said, thinking of the downsides of living and working in the same space that she faced every day. "This place would be perfect for that."

They passed the harbor. It was a calm day, so Stuart, Evan and Clyde had gone over to the island to do their reno work. Emily felt

22

very fortunate that the weather had been so mild. They definitely looked set to have everything finished for the April bookings. It was one less thing to worry about!

"Have you thought anymore about the babymoon?" Amy asked.

"Not really," Emily told her.

"You ought to go," Amy insisted. "You're almost out of time!" She nodded her head at Emily's ballooning stomach. Then she added, "There are some lovely hotels that do great babymoon packages."

Emily narrowed her eyes in suspicion. "Have you been researching?"

Amy grinned devilishly. "Just a little. Look in the pocket behind your seat."

Rolling her eyes jovially, Emily leaned around behind her and found a stack of glossy magazines. She heaved them out. "A little?" she joked.

"Okay, maybe a lot," Amy confessed. "I just really want you to have a break! My favorite one is on the top there. The spa in Quebec."

Emily looked at the first of Amy's selection. Located in the old part of Quebec city, it looked more like a castle than a hotel.

"It's right in the old center of town," Amy said. "So there's loads of culture and stuff. City walls. A citadel. Museums galore."

"Are you sure you don't want to go?" Emily joked, raising an eyebrow.

Amy laughed. "Of course I do. When it's my turn, that is. But my focus right now is the wedding and the house. When it's babymoon time, I'll be heading there, I promise." She leaned over and tapped the top of the magazine.

Emily glanced down again at the stunning castle. Maybe it wasn't such a bad idea. The babymoon package including a special prenatal massage for the mom's to be and a stress busting massage for the dad's to be. Plus all the products were natural, with no harmful chemicals, and all the food was organic. It did seem idyllic. Doctor Arkwright would certainly approve of Emily reducing her stress levels. Better late than never!

"Daniel will probably come up with a very logical and practical reason why we shouldn't go," Emily said. She listed on her fingers. "Chantelle. The island. My impending due date. To name just a few." But she slipped the magazine in her purse anyway to show him later. Maybe she could convince him.

They pulled onto the drive of the first viewing. Emily loved it immediately. The outside lawn was large with a hedge for them extra privacy, and there was enough space for at least two cars to park outside. The house was even more pretty in real life. There was a cute porch out the front, not quite as grand as the inn's wraparound one, but there was space for a rocking chair and bistro table with chairs.

"I can already tell I'm going to love it," Emily said.

But Amy didn't look so convinced. "It's a bit underwhelming," she said.

"Are you crazy?" Emily gasped. "It looks like something from a movie!"

"Yes," Amy continued, in a distracted sort of voice. "A *boring* movie."

Emily rolled her eyes at Amy's perfectionism, but at the same time, she knew she shouldn't be so harsh. Amy's life had gone completely differently to Emily's. Her college dorm room business had succeeded and she'd bought her New York apartment while still in her early twenties. To Amy, home had always meant independence. Now it would mean domesticity. Emily had to admit that, for Amy's tastes, it was possibly a little too sensible. There was no elevator to negotiate, no traffic hum in the distance. In short, there was no challenge. If Amy was going to be happy in this new stage of her life, Emily realized, she was going to have to find an exceptional house, not just a lovely one.

*

After a long day of house viewing and wedding venue gazing, Emily needed a nap back at the inn. She was starting to get incredibly tired in these last few weeks of pregnancy, but knew that she'd just have to get used to it because when Baby Charlotte was born, it would only get worse!

She dozed in bed, drifting in and out of sleep, taking the opportunity of an empty house to let the dogs sleep on the end of the bed -- something that was usually forbidden. She perused the brochure for the Quebec spa, mulling over how she would spin the idea to Daniel. Then she remembered a promise she'd made Chantelle; to invite Papa Roy to Christmas.

She hadn't had the heart to tell Chantelle when she'd asked that her father hadn't been in contact for several days and that the voicemails she'd left for him had gone unanswered. In fact, she realized now, she hadn't had the heart to admit it to herself. She'd blanked it entirely, not wanting to even consider for a split second what it might mean; that her father had passed. Even now she refused to allow herself to truly consider it. He had Vladi, his close friend, to care for him, and she'd made the elderly Greek man promise to call if anything happened. She chose instead to believe that Roy was off on some adventure, having too much fun to notice the days ticking by.

She grabbed her laptop and wrote a quick email. The telephone approach was clearly not working, and even though he was far less responsive with emails, it seemed like a good idea to change tack.

Dear dad,

I called a couple of times but haven't heard back, which I assume means you're making the most of the Greek weather and boating with Vladi! Chantelle's been asking whether you'll come for Christmas. I know you made it clear that you didn't want to fly, especially not to somewhere as cold as Maine, but please do consider it. You know you're her favorite person in the world!

All my love,

Emily.

She hit send and realized her cheeks were wet with tears. She wiped them away.

As she put her laptop away, she heard the sound of the inn door closing. It was probably Lois coming to start her short shift on the reception desk, or Bryony to set herself up in her usual work station in the guest lounge and work on their winter advertisements. But then she heard footsteps coming up the stairs, heavy and fast, and recognized them as Daniel's immediately.

"Mogsy! Rain! Off the bed!" she said hurriedly, trying to shoo them away.

Too late. The door flew open.

"Hey honey!" Daniel cried, grinning from ear to ear.

"What are you doing home so early?" she asked, happily surprised but also guilty.

As if he hadn't a care in the world, Daniel waltzed in and sat on the end of the bed, idly petting Rain.

"Jack's in the woodshop this evening," he said as he ran his hand across her long ear. "We've had a huge order in for a fairy princess staircase for a bar mitzvah and, well you know Jack, any excuse to be at work rather than home."

"That whole retirement thing isn't really working out for him, is it?" Emily laughed, her gaze falling to the dog, then snapping back up to Daniel.

"Nope," Daniel chuckled in response.

Mogsy whined for attention, and he cupped her face in both his hands and kissed the dog on the crown of her head.

"Good thing you're opening your own shop soon," Emily said, still a little disconcerted that Daniel hadn't scolded her for letting the dogs on the bed. "Have you told him yet?"

"Not yet. But I honestly don't think he'll mind. It will give him an excuse to tell his wife that he has to go back to work. She might think of me as a villain for a while but Jack will probably be very grateful!"

"Please let's not be like that after thirty years of marriage."

Daniel chuckled. "No way. I can't see either of us ever retiring. Can you?"

"Good point," Emily said. She narrowed her eyes then, still unsure what was going no. "You're in a very good mood."

"Am I?"

"Yes. You haven't even mentioned the dogs on the bed."

Daniel startled then as if he hadn't even realized they were there. "Oh!" But he just shrugged. "It's time to collect Chantelle. Do you want me to do it? If you're not feeling so good?"

"No, no, I want to come," Emily replied. "Who knows how many school pickups I'll miss once Charlotte's born. Think of Suzanna and Baby Robin. I hardly ever see her these days. I want to make the most of things right now, as they are."

He helped her to her feet. Emily felt very groggy, like her nap had achieved nothing.

They headed downstairs, Daniel holding Emily's hand for her as she took careful steps. It was amazing how much more daunting it felt to negotiate a large staircase now that she was fit to burst. To think not that long ago she'd been trotting up and down these steps with ease! Now they looked very steep.

Outside the weather was even miler that it had been that morning.

"How was the trip with Amy?" Daniel asked as he helped her into her seat.

"Great. She didn't like any of the three gorgeous houses we saw now any of the extraordinary wedding venues. But, that reminds me, she's found this babymoon spa for us in Quebec. I know you probably won't want to go but maybe we could think about it."

"What's to think about?" he exclaimed. "Let's do it!"

Now Emily really was surprised. Usually Daniel took a bit of convincing. She'd clearly caught him in a great mood.

"Are you feeling okay?" she asked, only half joking.

"I'm feeling just fine," Daniel replied, laughing. "I'm just happy to have been given a little bit of extra time with my wife this evening, that's all."

"That's very sweet," Emily relied, touched that her presence could cause him such happiness. "So you really want to go on a babymoon?"

"Sure," he said, shrugging. "As long as Chantelle doesn't mind. Hey, how about we take her out on the boat this afternoon to soften the blow? It is 60 degrees after all!"

"I thought Clyde, Stu and Evan were working on the island today. Don't they have it?"

Daniel shook his head. "They're using the hire trawler today. They've taken it along the coast to Beals. There's a great building supply company there but the materials are far too heavy for the cuddy cabin. Which means it's free for us."

"In that case we'll have to," Emily agreed. She loved boat trips, too, and any chance to see the island was welcome considering the weather could turn at any moment. It did seem like a stroke of luck that the opportunity had presented itself. Emily would be a fool to turn it down!

They made it to the school, parking up in the lot before getting out the truck. A moment later the doors burst open and children hurried down the steps. Chantelle appeared, her eyes scanning the parking lot for Emily's car. But instead she found the pickup truck, and by her expression, it was clear that she was thrilled to see her father unexpectedly picking her up. She ran towards them.

"Daddy," Chantelle cried, barrelling into his open arms. "What are you doing here?"

"Taking my special girl on a boat trip to our island, that's what," Daniel said. "What do you say to that? Want to go on a boat trip?"

"YES!" Chantelle exclaimed, jumping up and down.

She quickly ran back to the playground to say goodbye to her friends, before bolting back to the truck and jumping in.

"Wow, that was quick," Emily commented. She patted her stomach. "I miss being able to run like that!"

"Poor mommy," Chantelle said. "Not too long now. She'll be here before Christmas. Ooh, that reminds me. Did you speak to Papa Roy about coming for Christmas?"

Emily felt a jolt of anguish in her chest. What was the best thing to tell the girl? She didn't want her to worry unnecessarily.

"I sent him an email," Emily told her. "But why don't we try to call him when we're on the island?"

Chantelle nodded and settled down for the rest of the journey to the harbor.

When they arrived, everything was very quiet. In spite of the calm weather, most people had already packed up their boats for the winter. It was only because of the island renovation work that Daniel's boat was still out at all. It had been a stroke of luck, or fate aligning, that meant they'd been able to sail it so regularly.

Daniel jumped down into the boat first, before helping Chantelle and Emily in. Then they set off, cutting through the sparkling water in the direction of the island.

"Chantelle," Emily said, addressing the girl. "How would you feel if daddy and I went on a weekend trip just the two of us?"

Chantelle hesitated, her lips twisting to the side in thought.

"You can be honest," Daniel added. "We want to know how you really feel. Because there have been some times before when you've said okay but it's actually made you very sad."

Emily thought of her previous meltdowns. She hoped Chantelle didn't feel attacked by Daniel's comments and understood they were coming from a place of concern and love.

"I suppose it depends on who babysits me," Chantelle said, thoughtfully.

"Who would you like?" Emily asked.

"I'm happiest when I have a sleepover with my friends," she explained, sounding more mature than ever. "With Bailey and Toby. And also I prefer it to be short. After two nights I start to get worried."

"Okay," Emily said, nodding, pleased with how well Chantelle was able to articulate her feelings and needs now. "So shall I see if I can arrange a sleepover with either Yvonne or Suzanna? And only stay away for the weekend?"

"I think that would be okay," Chantelle said with a nod.

To Emily's great amusement, Chantelle held her hand out to shake Emily's. Emily took her hand and gave it a hearty shake.

"Deal!"

Just then, they reached the island and Emily saw the trawler Daniel had mentioned moored beside the gorgeous new jetty. Even though it hadn't been a particularly long time since they'd last been here, Emily was still very excited to see the progress to the cabins. The main structures were now complete, and even some of the landscaping work had started. It was so exciting to see everything coming together. And a relief too, since their income at the moment was relying on the island! Stu, Clyde and Evan had really surpassed her expectations and the company Daniel had employed to manage the project really were fantastic.

"I'd better go and check in with the guys," Daniel said, looking in the direction of the sound of sawing and hammering. "See how it went today with that new building supplies company. I'll be back in a minute."

He went off towards the cabins.

Emily and Chantelle settled down on the rocks, looking out to sea. The water was calm today, and the sight of the Maine coastline looked very beautiful. It was a tranquil moment, a slice of peace within an otherwise hectic life.

"Can we call Papa Roy now?" Chantelle asked after a moment. "You know we haven't spoken to him in three days now."

So Chantelle had noticed, Emily realized. Of course she had. The child was extremely observant, and the fact that she and her father's daily calls had ceased had not gone unnoticed.

"Do you think he's okay?" Chantelle asked.

Emily felt a heaviness weigh on her shoulders.

"I think he is," she told Chantelle. "I just think he's slipped back into an old habit."

Though Roy had promised to stay in touch, Emily knew old habits died hard, and there were still times when her efforts would be met by radio silence from him. It stung just as much now as it had when she was younger, when his long, slow disengagement from the family had begun following Charlotte's death. He'd drifted away from her bit by bit then and as a scared, confused child she'd just let it happen. Not anymore. She had a right to her father, to demand him to be in her life, to share with him her life and expect to hear the same from him.

She took her cell phone out and dialled his number. She listened to it ring and ring. There was no answer. She tried again, aware of Chantelle watching pensively from the corner of her eye. Each new attempt she made to get in touch with him made her stomach twist with anguish. On the fifth attempt, she slung the phone down into her lap.

"Why won't he answer?" Chantelle asked, her voice sad and frightened.

Emily knew she had to put on a brave face for the child but it was a real struggle. "He's asleep a lot," she said, weakly.

"Not for three days straight," Chantelle replied. "He should check his phone when he wakes up and see he's missed your calls."

"He might not have thought to check," Emily told him, attempting a reassuring smile. "You know what he's like with technology."

But Chantelle was too smart for Emily's excuses and she didn't rise to her feeble attempt at humor. Her expression remained serious and sullen.

"Do you think he's died?" she asked.

"No!" Emily exclaimed, feeling anger take off the edge of her worry. "Why would you say such an awful thing?"

Chantelle seemed surprised by Emily's outburst. Her eyes were wide with shock.

"Because he's very ill," she said meekly. "I just meant..." Her voice faded away.

Emily took a breath to calm herself. "I'm sorry, Chantelle. I didn't mean to snap like that. I get very worried when I haven't heard from Papa Roy in a while and what you said would be my worst nightmare."

Roy. Alone. Dead in bed with no one beside him. She cringed at the thought, her heart clenching.

Chantelle looked tentatively at Emily. She seemed unsure of herself, as though she was treading on eggshells, worried that Emily would erupt at her again.

"But there's no way for us to know, is there? Whether he's still alive?"

Emily forced herself to be the grown up Chantelle needed her to be, even though each question stung like a fresh wound being sluiced. "We know he's alive because Vladi is taking care of him. And if Vladi hasn't called then nothing is wrong. That was the deal, remember?"

In her mind she conjured up the weather-beaten tanned face of Vladi, the Greek fisherman her father had struck up a friendship with. Vladi had promised to keep her informed of Roy's condition, even if Roy himself wanted his deterioration to be kept from her. Whether Vladi kept good on his promise was another thing, though. Who would he be more loyal too, anyway; her, a young woman he'd known for a few days, or his lifelong friend Roy?

"Mommy," Chantelle said softly. "You're crying."

Emily touched her cheek and found it was wet with tears. She wiped them with her sleeve.

"I'm scared," she told Chantelle. "That's why. I miss Papa Roy so much. I just wish we could convince him to be here with us."

"Me too," Chantelle said. "I want him and Nana Patty to live in the inn. It's sad that they're so far away."

30

Emily reached her arm around her daughter and held her tightly. She could hear Chantelle gently sobbing and felt awful for her part in the child's unhappiness. Crying in front of her was never the plan. But it some ways she wondered whether it helped Chantelle to see her mother's emotions, to see that it was okay to be weak sometimes, to be scared and worried. The child had spent so many years of her life having to be strong and brave, perhaps seeing her mom cry would show her it was okay to let go of control sometimes.

"Why do people have to die?" Chantelle said then, her voice muffled by the way her face was pressed into Emily's chest.

"Because..." Emily began, before pausing and thinking very deeply about it. "I think because their spirit has elsewhere to be."

"You mean Heaven?" Chantelle asked.

"It could be Heaven. It could be somewhere else entirely."

"Daddy doesn't believe in that," Chantelle said. "He says no one knows whether you go somewhere after you die, and that in Judaism it's up to God to decide whether you get an afterlife or not."

"That's what daddy believes," Emily told her. "But you can believe whatever you want to. I believe something different. And that's okay too."

Chantelle blinked through her wet eyelashes, her big blue eyes on Emily. "What do you believe?"

Emily paused and took a long time to formulate her answer. Finally she spoke. "I believe there is somewhere that we go to after we pass, not in our bodies, they stay here on earth, but our spirits rise up and go to the next place. When Papa Roy gets there he will be so, so happy." She smiled, comforted by her own beliefs. "There'll be no more pain for him at all or ever again."

"No pain at all?" Chantelle's sweet voice sang. "But what will it feel like?"

Emily pondered the question. "I think it will feel like that moment when you take a bite of your favorite food all the time."

Chantelle looked at her through her tearstained lashes and giggled. Emily continued.

"Like eating chocolate cake forever but never getting sick. Each bite just as great as the last. Or like that feeling you get when you step back from something you've been working on for months and see your accomplishment and realize that *you* made it."

"Like my clock?" the little girl asked.

Emily nodded. "Exactly. And it's the perfect kind of warm, like being in the jacuzzi at the spa."

"Does it smell of lavender like the spa?"

"Yes! And there are rainbows."

"What about animals?" Chantelle asked. "It wouldn't be any fun if there weren't any animals to pet and play with."

"If you think there should be animals," Emily told her, "Then there are animals."

Chantelle nodded. But her smile soon faded and she returned to her pensive expression. "That's just make believe though. We don't really know."

Emily hugged her tightly. "No. No one does. No one can. All we have is what we believe. What we choose to believe. And I believe that that is what's waiting for Papa Roy. And it's what your aunt Charlotte has, too. And she looks down at us whenever she wants to, and sends us little signs so we know she's thinking of us. Papa Roy will do the same when the time comes."

"I'll miss him," Chantelle said. "Even if he does go to somewhere warm and happy, I'll miss him being here."

For all her reassurances about the afterlife, Emily couldn't help what she felt deeply inside. That she would still be left alone, to live out her life without him. He would be gone from her forever and though for him it would be a wondrous step into the unknown, for her it would mean pain and loneliness and misery.

She squeezed Chantelle tightly.

"I'll miss him too."

CHAPTER FOUR

Lights from the town hall spilled down the steps as Emily ascended them. Even from here she could hear numerous voices coming from inside. It sounded like the whole town might have turned up to hear the zoning board's decision about Raven's Inn. It shouldn't surprise Emily that every local would come. Even with the late announcement and the scheduling so soon after Thanksgiving, the people of Sunset Harbor cared so much about their town to make the time to attend all meetings.

She opened the door and saw that every available seat was taken. Raven Kingsley was all the way at the front, chatting with Mayor Hansen and his aide, Marcella. That didn't bode well, Emily thought to herself. If Raven had got them on her side it would only be a matter of time before the rest of the town were turned over as well.

She felt a tug on her arm and turned to see Amy and Harry.

"I'm so glad you came," Amy said. "There's been some rumblings in the underground that Raven's going to get the go ahead today. The zoning board aren't going to challenge her tearing down the old house in favor for something more modern. It looks like it will all come down to the residents."

"We have to fight this," Harry said. "A hotel could spell disaster for the inn, and my restaurant. Who's going to want to come all the way to our side of the harbor when there's somewhere newer and cheaper in a more central location? With ocean views? Think of all those random business bookings we get at the moment. We'd lose *all* that custom, I'm sure."

Harry's concerns made Emily worry even more than she had previously. She didn't want to stand in the way of Raven, especially after she'd confided in her about her bitter divorce. But she couldn't just stand by and have her own livelihood destroyed in such a manner. Raven, from all she'd heard, wasn't the type to take any prisoners. She had that ruthless New York business mentality - kill or be killed. Emily wasn't much of a fighter. She really could've done with Trevor by her side right now!

"I don't know what I'm supposed to do," Emily told them. "I don't want to stop her from doing her job just because I'm scared."

"Then do it for your family," Harry said. "For your friends and town. No one wants an ugly building on our oceanfront, and we don't want our beloved inn to go out of business either. It's not good for anyone."

"How are most people voting?" Emily asked.

Amy pointed to the corner, at the Patels. "Against, of course." Then over to the Bradshaws. "Against." She pointed next to Birk and Bertha. Birk owned the gas station and was the first person Emily had met in Sunset Harbor. "I think they're for. More cars coming in to town means more customers, as far as they're concerned."

Emily chewed her lip in consternation. The reality of a new rival inn arriving in town was starting to feel very real to her. The way Mayor Hansen was guffawing at something Raven had just said made her feel even worse.

Harry nudged her then. "Look, the meeting's about to start."

She turned towards the stage and the small wooden podium. The room fell silent as Mayor Hansen took his position. He banged his gavel, unnecessarily considering everyone was already paying him their undivided attention.

"Welcome everyone," he said. "We're here for the postponed discussions about Raven Kingsley's proposition to clear the dilapidated ocean side lot and build a new hotel there. You may or may not know already that the zoning board met earlier this week and voted unanimously for the plans to go ahead."

Emily looked at Harry and Amy. They were both grimacing. Emily felt her own face mirroring their expressions.

Mayor Hansen carried on. "Of course, we're a small town and the views of our residents are as equally important as the zoning boards. More so, in fact, now that we've lost our dear friend Trevor Mann."

He pressed a hand to his heart. There was a light-hearted ripple of laughter through the audience as everyone recalled Trevor's fierce, sometimes menacing protectiveness over the town.

"I believe many of you had a chance to speak to Raven over the thanksgiving break," Mayor Hansen finished. "So I'm looking forward to hearing all of your opinions. I suggest we here from Emily Morey first, since a new inn would have the greatest impact on her. Emily, would you like to take the floor?"

All eyes turned to her. Emily felt that familiar sensation of being put on the spot. And she really was in a bind. She didn't want to trash Raven's dream just because it might make things a little trickier for her. It wasn't in her spirit. But at the same time, Harry and Amy's tense expressions from beside her reminded her that there were people counting on her. All her staff, her family. They'd expanded the inn massively, having the luxury of no competition. At the very least Raven's new venture would mean some cut backs for Emily's inn, including staff reductions.

"I…" Emily began, feeling her throat becoming dry.

She looked over at Raven sitting on the stage beside Marcella. For only the second time since she'd met her, Emily saw a genuine smile on her face. Like Emily when she'd first arrived, Raven had encountered hostility and suspicion from the locals. Emily was probably the one person she counted as a friendly acquaintance.

"I'm for," Emily suddenly blurted. "I think there's a market that Raven's inn could capture. She caters for the business and corporate end of the market, with conferences and the like. I cater more towards familie, weddings and festivities. There's room for the both of us."

She spoke very quickly, trying to get her explanation out before her voice was entirely swallowed by the uproar. But it was useless. Everyone was speaking loudly over one another, directing frustration towards her, as if she were the one who'd come up with the plan in the first place, rather than the person who was going to be the most affected by it should it come to fruition!

And even worse were the thunderous expressions on Harry and Amy's faces. They looked like she'd just said the worst thing in the world, like she'd let them down terribly. But it just wouldn't be right or fair to sway everyone to her side, to tell Raven no. It would be downright mean spirited.

All she could do now was hope that enough other people voted no so she wouldn't have to deal with the outcome of her generosity.

Emily stepped back, seeking the shadows. But in a small town like Sunset Harbor there was no hiding. She'd made her bed, now she would have to lie in it.

*

"What the Hell was that, Emily?" Amy demanded once the town meeting was over. "Anyone would think you wanted to go bankrupt and ruin the town!"

Her friend had let her go less than five paces from the town hall before launching her attack, stopping her on the first step. The weather had grown colder since they'd been inside and Emily shivered from the sudden drop in temperature.

But despite the cold, her cheeks were warm with embarrassment. Emily hated making a public scene, especially since half of the town were filling out of the hall behind them.

"Can we talk about this later?" Emily said under her breath.

"No!" Amy exclaimed. "I want to know what's gotten into you. Why are you lying down like a lapdog for Raven Kingsley?"

"That's hardly what's happening," Emily refuted, stung by the ferocity of Amy's words. "Just because I don't want to trash her dreams doesn't mean I'm bending over backwards to accommodate her."

Amy placed her hands on her hips. "Funny, 'cos it's certainly coming across that way. I mean just the other day you were telling me all your woes about laying off staff over winter and not having any bookings. What do you really think will happen when you have a competitor like Raven Kinsgley offering cheaper rooms, cheaper food, a better location? You may as well just fire Harry now."

"Ames, please calm down," Emily said, softly. She tried to reach for her friend, but Amy pulled away. She wasn't a crier, never had been, but Emily noticed that her face was red from the strain of holding it together.

"I just don't understand you," Amy said, turning her face away. "I don't understand what you're doing."

Emily had no words. It was hard to explain herself, beyond the fact that she wanted to be a decent human being and spread kindness. She'd seen the way Chantelle had resolved her issue with Laverne over Halloween and had been humbled by the child's capacity for care and forgiveness. The only may she could make sense of it now was that dragging someone wasn't right, no matter what.

"Even the Raven Kingsley's of the world deserve a chance," Emily said. "I'm sorry if you feel like I've betrayed Harry, or even that I'm letting myself and my family down, but I simply cannot stoop to that level, to trash someone's dream like that."

Amy stared at her, still incredulous, like her words just weren't registering. "I think you're going to regret that. Once Raven drives you out of business."

"How about when that happens, you can say 'I told you so,'" Emily said, the comment halfway between a joke and a dismissal.

Amy shook her head, looking beyond disappointed. It was painful for Emily to have her best friend so mad at her, but she wasn't going to back down under the pressure. She knew what was right in her heart and that was the only thing was going to let that guide her actions.

"I'm going home," Amy said.

"No, Ames," Emily said, reaching for. "It's the tree lighting ceremony. Your first one in Sunset Harbor. Come on, let's just put this behind us for the rest of the night, okay?"

Amy shook her head again. "I can't. I'm sorry. I don't feel like watching a stupid tree ceremony when our livelihoods are in danger. Doesn't feel like much to celebrate." She looked around her, searching for Harry.

Emily felt crushed. She and Amy had had their fair share of spats during their years of friendship but this particular one felt very raw and painful. Amy's rejection hurt.

Harry appeared then, moving away from a very solemn looking conversation with the Bradshaw's who owned a restaurant in town. He came over, his usual boyish grin completely absent, and placed his arm around Amy.

"Shall we go home?" he asked her, his tone morose.

Emily's heart sank. "Harry, come on," she said. "It's the tree lighting. Come over to the Inn for mulled wine, then we can all go together."

But Harry shook his head. He was hardly looking at her. "I think we want a quiet night in."

Amy didn't raise her eyes again either. Instead, the two of them shuffled off, heads bowed, leaving Emily alone on the steps, watching them go with a downturned mouth.

*

After her spat with Amy, Emily couldn't help but approach the town tree lighting celebration with an air of trepidation. What if everyone decide to give her a piece of them mind as Amy had? The thought of the tense atmosphere that had built during the meeting spilling onto the streets and poisoning the joyful celebration was a real concern.

But when they arrived and climbed out of Daniel's truck -- Chantelle clipping leashes onto the dogs before hopping down from the back seat -- Emily quickly realized she needn't have worried. All she saw were the same old friendly faces, smiles and greetings. Whatever feelings the locals felt about her speech at the meeting, it appeared as if they were going to put them aside for the rest of the evening. Unlike Amy, they seemed willing to leave their animosity towards her within the four walls of the town hall.

In typical Sunset Harbor tradition, the tree lighting wasn't just a tree lighting, but instead a street party, an excuse to celebrate.

Emily looked around at all the stalls that had been set up, selling an assortments of winter-themed items from Christmas decorations to candles, flavored liquors and ugly Christmas sweaters. Chantelle, of course, was immediately drawn to the sparkly, garish sweater stall.

"We should all get one of these!" she exclaimed with excitement, picking up a bright-green sweater made to look like a uniform for Santa's elves. "What do you think? Daddy, you suit green."

Daniel looked at Emily with an amused expression. "But do I suit it better than red, is the real question?" he asked, holding up a sweater designed to look like a fireplace complete with shiny flames.

Chantelle immediately discarded her elf sweater and cooed at the shiny fabric. "Okay this one is better. We should get one for Nana Patty incase she comes. And one for Papa Roy, too, because you never know, and I don't want him to feel left out."

Emily felt a stab of grief in her chest at the mention of her father. She was certain he'd not come to Christmas, even when he did finally pick up her calls. He'd made it quite clear in his previous letters that he wanted to remain independent, to live out his remaining days in the hillsides of Greece rather than wasting his time traveling back and forth across the globe, or enduring a cold winter in Maine. Emily recalled now one of the comments he'd written in one of the letters she'd recently received. It was a bittersweet one, poignant enough to be committed immediately to memory. *'Should I mind that I've almost certainly seen my last snowflake? Because I do not! If my days are numbered, I'd like nothing more than for every single last one of them to be sunny."*

"Can we, mommy?" Chantelle said, breaking through her thoughts.

Emily cleared her mind and looked down to discover that Chantelle had found a new, gaudy collection of Christmas sweaters, this time with sequined reindeers on a backdrop of candy cane stripes..

"Of course," she said, smiling. "Let's get those."

"And the elf ones for Evan, Stu and Clyde," Chantelle added, with a decisive nod. "They're daddy's little helpers after all."

Emily laughed. "Great idea."

They bought the sweaters and Emily put them away in her bag. She spotted Owen then, and waved. He came over, smiling shyly. Once he reached them, Chantelle hugged him.

"So have you and Serena started packing?" Emily asked, trying to remain enthusiastic about their move to Singapore, rather than sad for herself to be losing two such wonderful friends.

"Not yet," Owen replied. "We're not leaving until the New Year."

"Good," Emily said, relieved. "It would be awful if you didn't get to meet Baby Charlotte."

"I agree."

"Hey, Owen," Chantelle said, gazing up at him from where she was hanging around his waist. "Did you know we're doing A Seussified Christmas Carol this year for our Christmas show?"

"You are?" Owen said, looking excited. "That's a great one!"

"Maybe I could have a few singing lessons with you?" Chantelle asked. "I know you're not my teacher anymore but it would be really nice to practice with you a couple of times, like we did last year with the nutcracker."

Emily spoke up then. "Love, Owen's very busy at the moment."

"I don't mind," Owen said. "I mean, I'd love to. Honestly. When is the production?"

"Friday 18th," Emily said.

"Isn't that the same night as Roman's cocktail party?" Owen asked.

Emily shook her head, recalling the pretty invitation from Roman that was pinned to the corkboard in the study. "That's on the Thursday. It's going to be a busy week!"

"Sure is," Owen laughed. "Well anyway, if we did one lesson a week, we'd be able to fit in three before the performance day. How does that sound?"

Emily thought he looked genuinely pleased to have a few more lessons with Chantelle before he left for good. And Chantelle, of course, looked thrilled.

"Yes please!" she cried. "And you'll come and see the performance as well?" Chantelle asked.

"I wouldn't miss it for the world," Owen told her.

Just then, they noticed the crowds were moving, facing in the direction of the stage that was set up in front of the twenty foot Christmas tree. Roman and Mayor Hansen were climbing the steps.

"What's Roman doing up there?" Chantelle asked, giggling.

"I think he's the special guest," Emily replied, laughing also. It seemed so strange now that they knew Roman personally to think of him as a famous pop star, the sort that turned up for Christmas Tree lighting celebrations!

Mayor Hansen started speaking into the microphone and silence fell. Then there was a sudden gasp of noise as everyone realized that snowflakes were falling from the sky. All eyes turned upwards, distracted completely.

"Excuse me," Mayor Hansen said, frowning. But then his expression changed, and he turned his eyes up also, watching the first snowfall of winter.

There was a moment of perfect silence, like the snow had paused everything. Emily felt in that moment as if she were floating, as if each fluttering snowflake brought peace with it. It was a beautiful moment, made even better when she felt Daniel scoop her and Chantelle in his arms, pulling them into him protectively.

"Well, I've never been upstaged by ice before," Roman's voice said over the microphone.

Everyone in the crowd laughed, and soon people's eyes were turning back to the tree, to the stage and the celebrations.

"Happy Christmas everyone," Roman said. "Will you count with me? Three!"

Everyone joined in.

"TWO! ONE!"

Roman hit the big, red button. In a burst of twinkling color, the tree lit up. There was a collective gasp followed by rapturous applause.

"It's so pretty," Chantelle exclaimed.

"And so lucky they'd cut it down before the fire," Owen added.

Emily looked over at him, frowning. "What do you mean? What fire?"

"Didn't you hear?" Owen said, turning his eyes away from the beautiful tree and looking at Emily, shocked. "Terry's Christmas Tree farm. There was a huge fire out there. Burned everything to the ground. Even his house."

Emily gasped. "But we were there just the other day! I don't believe it."

Jason, the local firefighter, was standing a little way ahead of them and he turned then and addressed Emily in a hushed voice.

"We got called up there," he said. "It was that much of a blaze that they needed to call on other local crews to help. Such a tragedy. His whole business and his home destroyed right before Christmas. And you know he's got no family in the area. Never married. No kids."

"Where is he staying?" Emily asked, feeling greatly saddened by the shocking news.

Jason told her; "He's in a hostel, I think. Temporary emergency accommodation until he can make other arrangements. What those other arrangements will be, though, I've no idea..."

"We'll have to put him up at the inn," Emily said immediately. "We can't leave him in a hostel for Christmas!"

She looked to Daniel appealingly.

"Of course," Daniel said without missing a beat. "We have the space. The more the merrier."

"Do you have a way we can get in touch with him?" Emily asked Jason.

"Of course," Jason said. "If you call the fire department up there they should be able to put you in touch. Here." He scribbled the number down for her.

Emily wasted no time. She grabbed her cell phone and called the fire service division and got the number from them. Then she called the hostel where Terry was staying, and was put on hold as they went to find him.

"Hello?" came his voice over the other end of the phone, sounding confused and tired.

"Terry, this is Emily, the manager from the Inn at Sunset Harbor. We came and bought a tree of you just the other day."

"I can't do refunds," Terry said quickly. "My business is all up in the air at the moment and.. And..." He sounded close to tears.

"Oh no, you misunderstood," Emily told him, hurrying to rectify the situation. "We heard about the fire on your property and we wanted to offer you one of our rooms for the festive period."

There was a pause on the other end of the line. Emily wondered, suddenly, if she'd overstepped the mark. Terry lived alone with no family, after all. Perhaps he'd chosen that, in the same way her father had. By offering him a room, had she offended him by implying he was lonely?

But then Terry spoke.

"You'd do that?" he asked. He sounded stunned. "Really?"

"Absolutely," Emily said. "We have space and we love spending time with people. I mean, that's obvious. We wouldn't have opened an inn if we didn't! But honestly, we'd be delighted to have another guest."

"I... I don't think I'd be able to pay you anything," Terry stammered. "I mean, the business, I don't know what's going to happen with the insurance and how long it will take or whether I'll even be able to start again and..."

"You wouldn't have to pay a cent," Emily told him, interrupting his nervous monologue.

There was another long silence. Finally, in a voice that cracked with emotion, Terry replied, "I don't know what to say."

"How about, 'see you tomorrow'?" Emily suggested.

"Yes. Yes, okay. I'll see you tomorrow! Thank you, Emily!"

They ended the call, and Chantelle grinned up at her mom. "This is going to be the best Christmas ever," she said. Then suddenly a look of worry appeared on her face.

"What is it, honey?" Emily asked, concerned.

"Quick!" Chantelle cried, tugging on Emily's hand. "We have to get Terry a Christmas sweater!"

CHAPTER FIVE

Emily's mind was still reeling from the fight with Amy when she woke the next morning. Amy had been furious, and she could only hope that in time she'd calm down, because they certainly weren't going to ever see eye to eye on this issue. Time was the only healer in this case.

She got out of bed and went to look out her bedroom window. As she pulled back the curtain, she discovered a world of white awaiting her. Snow must have fallen all throughout the night, covering the yard, the trees, and all their neighbor's rooftops in a thick white blanket. Before she'd even had time to let go of the curtain, Chantelle sprung in through the bedroom door.

"SNOW DAY!" she cried.

Daniel sat up in bed abruptly. He'd still been sleeping. "What's going on?" he said, sounding panicked by the abrupt wake up call.

Chantelle leapt up on the bed. "SNOW DAY!" she cried.

Daniel sunk back, a hand across his heart. "Oh phew. You gave me a fright."

Emily ushered Chantelle off the bed. "How about we have some breakfast then get dressed in our warmest clothes, then go outside and make a snowman on the front lawn?"

Chantelle grinned and hurried away.

Emily went over to Daniel and kissed him lightly. "Sorry for your sudden wake up alarm," she told him.

He chuckled. "I wouldn't have it any other way."

Emily smiled down at him. "I'll go and put the coffee pot on."

She wrapped herself up in her nightgown and headed down the steps. Baby Charlotte was awake and she could feel her moving around, kicking her right in the ribs. Emily could feel her moving more and more every day now. She was also growing every day, by the looks of her continuously expanding belly! Surely it couldn't get any bigger?

When Emily entered the kitchen, she discovered that Stu, Evan and Clyde were there as well as Chantelle. Stu was making waffles, Evan was brewing coffee, and Clyde was patiently watching Chantelle as she explained her fiddly clock making.

"Good morning!" Stu cried, looking over his shoulder at Emily. "You're just in time for my special snow day waffles."

"And what are those?" Emily asked, smiling as she took a seat at the table.

"Cinnamon and blueberry," Stuart said. "Sound good?"

"Sounds amazing," Emily replied, licking her lips. Charlotte wriggled as if in agreement.

Clyde looked across the table. "Is it okay that we're not on the island today?" he asked. "With the weather and everything."

"Of course it's okay!" Emily cried. "It wouldn't be safe on the water today."

She thought suddenly of Terry. He was supposed to be heading to the inn today. She hoped the roads were clear and that he'd still be able to make it and not get stuck in that hostel because of the snow. Another night there would certainly be one night too many.

Chantelle glanced up from her clock then. "Besides, you have to help me make a snowman," she told Clyde. "It has to be the tallest snowman in the world and I won't be able to reach without you."

Emily chuckled as she thought of all the times Clyde had picked Chantelle up over his head. Now it was payback time!

Daniel came into the kitchen at last, ready to begin his day. Stu finished up the waffles and everyone came and sat at the kitchen table to eat.

"These are amazing!" Emily cried, tasting the delicious flavors, slathered in maple syrup. "I'll have to pass your recipe onto Matthew."

"Mmm, snow day waffles," Daniel said aloud. "I haven't eaten these for at least a decade!"

Everyone finished eating then went to get themselves ready for the day, washing, drying and dressing in several layers of warm clothing. Then they all congregated in the foyer.

Emily opened the door. A gust of icy air whirled in as the sight of crisp, white snow, at least a two foot deep, sparkled before their eyes. It was dazzling, the clear sky reflecting off the white surface like sunshine on glass.

"Wow," everyone murmured in awed appreciation.

The dogs hurried past Emily's legs, scurrying across the lawn and leaving pawprints across the otherwise unblemished surface. Chantelle went next, stomping and jumping around so she could make perfect foot prints.

Emily shoved her hands deep inside her pockets and stepped out onto the snowy porch. Her footsteps crunched as she took slow, careful steps.

From the other side of the lawn, Chantelle waved back at her.

44

"This is the perfect spot for our snowman!" she yelled. "We need as much snow here as possible."

"I'm on it," Stu cried, hurrying off to collect armfuls of snow for her. The other two joined suit.

Soon, Chantelle had an enormous pile of snow at her feet. Together, they molded and shaped it until the body of the snowman began to form.

"It needs to be bigger," Chantelle said, when it reached her height.

They kept going, piling more and more snow onto the body of the snowman. Emily's hands began to sting from the cold.

"Bigger!" Chantelle cried when it was as tall as Daniel.

"I don't know if we can go bigger," he said.

"Of course we can," Stu grinned. "We just need to get the ladder."

Chantelle laughed, clearly delighted that someone was joining in with her mischievous adventurousness. Stu ducked inside, then came back out with the ladder they'd used when decorated the tree. They'd be able to at least get eight feet with the help of the ladder, Emily thought.

Daniel held it steady while Chantelle climbed the ladder, then Stu, Evan and Clyde helped hand up snow for Chantelle to dump on the top. Meanwhile, Emily worked on the base, patting it down and making sure it was wide enough to support the additional weight going on the top.

When Chantelle could stretch no further she climbed down the ladder.

"Time to make the head," she announced.

She bent down and made a small snowball, then started rolling it across the ground, picking up fresh snow as she went. The ball started growing bigger. Daniel went to help her, providing some extra muscle. Chantelle laughed with delight as they pushed the snowball around, making it grow bigger and bigger and bigger. Then Stu joined them, followed by Clyde, and finally Evan. Emily watched, chuckling to herself, as they all ran around like children.

"I think that's big enough now," Chantelle finally announced. "Who's putting it on the top?"

"You are," Stu said.

Chantelle shook her head. "I can't. I already had to stretch my arms to get to the shoulders. Someone taller than me has to go." She looked at Daniel. "Daddy?"

Stu, Evan and Clyde began chanting, "Danny Boy! Danny Boy! Danny Boy!"

"This was way more than I bargained for," Daniel replied with resignation.

He climbed to the top of the ladder, Stu and Evan keeping it steady. Then Clyde lifted the large snowman head and handed it up to him. Daniel took it in his arms, clumsily, his tongue sticking out the side of his mouth with concentration. Then very, very slowly, he guided it up, rolling it across the body of the snowman until he could give it a final push onto the top. Then he patted it to make sure it wasn't going to roll straight off again.

"Done!" Daniel proclaimed.

Everyone clapped, proud of their achievement.

Daniel started climbing down the ladder when Chantelle cried, "Wait, daddy! We need to get things for the face."

She hurried off, then came back a little bit later with some pebbles for eyes and sticks to make a mouth. She passed them up to Daniel, who was waiting patiently, shivering, at the top of the ladder.

Daniel arranged the items into a cute, smiling face. Then finally, their handiwork was complete and he climbed back down, making it back to solid ground once more.

Emily stood back and admired their creation. It was a ten foot tall snowman, with the cutest, smiliest face imaginable.

"We need a picture for the website!" she exclaimed.

"Let me take it," Stu said. "Just the family."

Emily, Daniel and Chantelle stood beside the snowman and smiled as Stu took pictures on Emily's phone. Then he showed them the pictures.

"Our snowman looks amazing!" Chantelle cried, beaming from ear to ear.

"I'll email this to Bryony," Emily said. "Get her to put it on the website with a Christmas message from us all."

She typed a quick message and attached the photo then sent it off to Bryony. No sooner had the message sent, but her phone began to ring.

"It's Yvonne," she announced, and picked up the call.

But it wasn't Yvonne's voice on the other end. It was Bailey's.

"Hi Emily. Are you going to come ice skating with us?" Bailey asked, speaking at her usual mile a minute speed. "A bunch of us from school are going. My mom will be there, and Suzanna and Holly. Can you come?"

Emily smiled to herself. Bailey, like Chantelle, was one of life's natural leaders.

"We'd love to come," she said, although she wasn't sure she should be skating with her big whale belly. "We'll be there after lunch."

She hung up and looked at Chantelle and Daniel.

"We have a play date," she said. "At the ice rink."

Chantelle punched the air. "YES! I LOVE skating."

"Then let's warm up inside by the fire," Emily said. "I don't know about you guys but my fingers are frozen stiff."

Everyone laughed and headed back inside, leaving their giant snowman standing guard at the front of the inn.

*

The ice rink had been set up in the center of town and it looked absolutely stunning, surrounded by fairy lights and fake winter trees. Daniel pulled up into the lot. It was very busy, as if every single person in Sunset Harbor had decided this was the best way to make the most of the snow day.

"There's Yvonne," Emily said, pointing to where a group of parents were standing beside the perimeter of the rink, wrapped up in woolly clothes, holding a thermos and little cups that sent steam spiralling upwards. She noticed amongst them a white-blond haired, elegant woman. Realizing who it was, Emily added, "Oh, she's with Raven."

Daniel parked, and everyone got out the truck. They headed straight towards the group of parents. Yvonne must have noticed them approaching because she looked over and broke into a wide grin.

"Happy snow day!" she exclaimed, accepting the hug Chantelle gave her. Then she looked down at the girl. "Bailey and Laverne are already on the rink. Just over there."

She pointed to where the two girls were whizzing around, Bailey in her usual clumsy manner, Laverne looking like a pro-skater.

Chantelle looked extremely eager to join them. "Come on, Daddy. Can you help me get my boots on?"

Daniel took her by the hand and bade farewell to the group of moms, then he and Chantelle headed off towards the small kiosk where shoes could be exchanged for skates.

"How is everyone today?" Emily asked, looking back at the small group of parents. She was pleased to see Holly in attendance. She'd not been around as much since her tragic miscarriage on Halloween.

"Great," Yvonne said. "Here, have some hot chocolate."

She poured a small cup from the thermos and handed it to Emily. Emily accepted it gratefully. The warmth seeped through her gloves into her hands. Shame there was nothing she could use to warm her nose! It was stinging from the cold.

"Yvonne, I was hoping to ask you a favor," Emily said to her friend. "Daniel and I were thinking of going on a babymoon weekend trip. Chantelle said she wouldn't mind if she could have a sleep over at yours. Could we do that?"

"Of course!" Yvonne said. "You know we love having her over. Just tell me when."

Emily was so grateful for Yvonne's support. The babymoon really could go ahead now.

Raven turned to Emily then. "Thanks so much for what you did at the meeting," she said. "I really wasn't expecting you to stand up for me."

Emily blushed, and squirmed uncomfortably on the spot. She knew Raven wasn't the sort of woman who readily offered gratitude, so she nodded in affirmation.

"It wouldn't be fair otherwise," Emily said. "This town gave me a chance to make it. I'd be a real Scrooge if I didn't pass that goodwill on."

"Speaking of Scrooge," Yvonne said. "Who's looking forward to the Christmas show this year?"

"I can't wait," Holly said. "Dr Seuss is one of my childhood favorites. I've read all the books to Levi about a million times. He's just thrilled and can't wait to do his thing as Solicitor Number Two."

Everyone chuckled.

"Bailey is Sally Cratchit," Yvonne said, looking a little sullen. "I don't think she's too happy. What did Chantelle get?"

"She's the Ghost of Christmas Past," Emily said. "I think it's quite a big role. She showed me the script and songs the other day. It's pretty thick. I don't know when we're going to get the time to learn it all! But Owen said he'd do some extra lessons with her. Who's playing Scrooge?"

The mom's all looked from one face to the next. Finally, Raven spoke.

"It went to Laverne."

"Oh!" Emily exclaimed, thinking of the sullen little girl, who was always serious and rarely cracked a smile. Never had there been a more fitting casting. Quickly, she added, "It's the main part. Congratulations to Laverne."

48

Raven pursed her lips as if she was well aware of what they were all thinking.

Just then, Emily noticed that Chantelle and Daniel had made it onto the rink. They started skating around the perimeter, hand in hand, until they reached where the small group of parents were standing on the other side.

"Look at you go!" Emily cried at Chantelle. "You're very steady on your feet."

Daniel leaned over the barrier and kissed Emily. "Which is more than can be said for me! I'm feeling pretty wobbly up here."

"So guess what," Emily told Chantelle. "Yvonne has said you can have a sleepover with Bailey when we go away. Is that alright?"

"YAY!" Chantelle said. "I can't wait."

"You two can bake cookies and watch films," Yvonne said. "Sound good?"

Chantelle nodded. Then she looked over at Emily

"Are you going to come skating, mommy?" Chantelle asked.

Emily patted her stomach. "I don't think it would be a good idea. I'd hate to fall."

As if on cue, someone took a tumble. They landed with a heavy thud noise. One of the helpers skated over and got them back on their feet. They weren't hurt, but their pride was clearly damaged.

"See," Emily said. "Baby Charlotte would not be very pleased if I did that to her."

Chantelle pouted. "Maybe it would make her come out quicker."

Emily laughed. "I don't want her to come out quicker! I want her to stay cosy and warm inside for as long as she wants to."

"Have you passed the due date?" Yvonne asked.

"No, it's December 13th," Emily told her. "But my mom takes great delight in telling me I'll be at least two weeks late."

"Make it twelve days and you'll have a Christmas baby!" Yvonne added.

Daniel and Chantelle laughed at the prospect. Emily rubbed her stomach. It was all getting so close, becoming so real. Sooner or later, Baby Charlotte would be here to say hello.

*

That evening, the family spent some time in the living room, relaxing by the fire. Despite a busy day of snowmen building and ice skating, the downtime made Emily's mind turn to her father. She kept drifting off into wistful daydreaming. It didn't help that

49

Chantelle was drawing a picture on the floor before her with the giant words FOR PAPA ROY at the top of the paper.

She untucked her legs from beneath her and stood. "Maybe I should call Vladi."

Daniel looked at the clock. "It will be too late in Greece. Everyone will be sleeping."

"It's my last option," Emily replied.

Chantelle looked up at her, concern in her eyes. Daniel stood too, bringing an arm around Emily and leading her from the room so they could continue the conversation in private.

She faced him. "In the morning, then. I'll call Vladi first thing."

Daniel reached for her. "We did promise only to call Vladi in an emergency and vice versa."

"Doesn't this count?" Emily said. "Days of silence?"

"I honestly don't think it does. I know it's hard, but this is Roy's way. You know it, I know it. We don't have to like it. But it is what he does."

Emily knew what Daniel was saying was true, but she just couldn't quell her worry. "Maybe if I just spoke to Vladi I'd be able to calm down."

Daniel touched her bump tenderly. "If it will help put your mind at rest, then it would be for the best. But I don't think it's necessary, personally. I thinkk Roy's just gone off the radar, like he does. It doesn't matter how many voicemails you leave or emails you send, or how many times you call Vladi and hear that Roy's okay. Worrying won't make him get in contact any quicker. If it could, we wouldn't have spent twenty years wondering where he was."

Emily didn't like thinking of those times during which her father was deemed missing. The only good to come of them was that it brought she and Daniel closer. Since Roy had been a father figure to Daniel, his disappearance had been just as painful for him as it had for her, and they were the only two people in the world who shared that particular pain.

"Try to think of the baby," Daniel said. "The stress won't be good for her."

"You're right," Emily said.

She vowed to push it from her mind tonight at the least. Tomorrow, if she still felt this awful, she would speak to Vladi.

"Come on," Daniel said. "Let's make dinner. That might help take your mind off things."

They went to the kitchen and cooked together. Emily realized Danie was right. The task was relaxing, and the more she occupied herself, the less she worried.

Soon, they were all sat together in the dining room, slurping chicken stew. They'd just finished seconds when the doorbell rang.

"Will that be Owen?" Chantelle asked, with a yawn.

She seemed far too exhausted for a singing lesson, Emily thought.

"Maybe," she said, discarding her napkin on the table and standing. "Although he's a little early. I'll go let him in."

She left the dining room and walked through the foyer to the front door. But when she opened it, it was not Owen waiting on the steps for her, but a face she recognized but could not place. An older man, stubbly gray hair on his chin, deep-set lines across his forehead.

"Terry?" Emily said. "I didn't recognize you!"

She realized as she said it the reason why; she'd only ever seen him with a smile on his face.

"Evening. Sorry I'm so late. It wasn't so easy to get a taxi driver with the roads like they are."

Emily blushed, realizing she'd quite forgotten he was coming.

"Come in. Would you like some food? We've just had dinner so can easily fix you up a plate." She looked over her shoulder and called in the direction of the dining room. "Daniel? Can you come and help with Terry's bags?"

She looked back and smiled at Terry as he stepped out of the cold, dark evening and into the warmth of the inn. He had an embarrassed look on his face, like he was worried he was already a nuisance. Emily saw then that he had no bags. Terry had arrived with nothing but the clothes on his back. Her heart ached for him.

Daniel appeared behind her, Chantelle hovering beside him, shy but excited to meet their guest.

"Can you fix Terry up some food?" Emily asked Daniel.

"Of course," Daniel said, smiling kindly. "I hope you like chicken stew, Terry. We've got a vat of the stuff!"

"That's very kind," Terry said, and Emily could hear his voice hitch with emotion.

"Come into the lounge," she said, guiding him towards the door. "We're going to get a fire going and then Chantelle's singing teacher will be over to help her learn some songs for her Christmas show."

"How delightful," Terry said. "Back before I was a Christmas tree farmer, I had plans to be a singer."

"You did?" Chantelle asked, her eyes widening.

"Oh yes," Terry replied. "I had a little guitar I'd take out onto the street corners and I'd sing Elvis classics. I was a proud young man then. I was certain I'd get to be famous one day."

He saw the piano in the corner of the room then, Roy's antique one that Emily had had restored when she first arrived at the inn.

"Gosh, she's a beauty isn't she," Terry said. "May I?"

"Please," Emily said, gesturing with her hand.

She took a seat at the round table in the window and looked over at him as he took his position. Chantelle stood right beside the piano, clearly wanting to be as close to the action as possible.

Terry played a chord, softly, then another, as if reacquainting himself with the sensation. Then he played a simple melody with his right hand. Emily recognized the tune. *Have Yourself A Merry Little Christmas.* It was one of her favorites, though it always brought a sense of melancholy with it, she thought. Her father had sung it too, when she was younger, at that very piano, and she thought of him now, her heart skipping with emotion.

Terry brought his left hand up to the bass notes, and instead of playing the tune now, he played the accompaniment. A rich, warm sound filled the living room, and it was followed swiftly by Terry's own voice as he began to sing the words. He really was an amazing singer. His big-headedness in youth had been justified!

Daniel came in holding tray. On it was a bowl of stew for Terry and four steaming mugs of his special tea. He stopped in the doorway, watching, as if spell-bound by the song. Chantelle looked up at him and grinned. She, more than anyone, seemed enamored by Terry's talent.

Terry reached the last line of the song, and slowed the tempo just slightly. "So have yourself a merry little Christmas day…" The final word rang out, painful in its beauty.

Terry stopped, and removed his hands from the piano. There was a stunned silence. Then finally, Emily began to clap.

"Amazing," she said.

Chantelle threw her arms around Terry's neck. "That was awesome!" she yelled.

Terry laughed and patted her arms shyly.

She let go. "Terry, once Owen moves to Singapore, will you be my new singing teacher?"

"Chantelle," Emily said in her warning voice. "Give Terry at least five minutes to settle in before you bombard him."

"And let him eat his dinner," Daniel added, holding up the tray.

Terry stood and came over to the table. He accepted the dinner from Daniel. Daniel and Chantelle took the other two seats, and everyone took a mug of tea from the tray.

"What is your Christmas play this year, Chantelle?" Terry asked.

"A Seussified Christmas Carol," she told him. "I'm the Ghost of Christmas Past. I have a solo. Owen's coming over to help me practise."

"I can't wait to hear your voice," Terry said, munching on a spoonful of stew. "I saw you sing once in church."

"You did?" Chantelle asked, looking excited.

"Yes. You have a very lovely voice."

Chantelle beamed with pride.

Daniel went over to the hearth to light a fire and soon the room was filled with warm, orange light. Then the bell rang again.

"That will be Owen," Daniel said.

He went to answer the door, and a few moments later returned to the living room with Owen in tow.

"Terry," Owen said when he saw the older gentleman at the window table. He extended a hand. "I'm happy to see you. Such terrible news. Are you alright?"

Terry struggled to hold back the tears as he shook Owen's hand. "I've been offered food and a bed by Emily. Now I'm about to be serenaded by Chantelle. I'd say things are looking up."

Owen went over to the piano and took out the sheet music for Chantelle's play.

They'd practiced the song a few times when a clattering noise came from the foyer. Emily immediately knew it was Evan, Stu and Clyde returned home from the bar. Somehow they always managed to make a lot of noise.

"Are we having a Christmas sing-a-long?" Stu asked, poking his head around the door.

Owen looked at Chantelle. "What do you say? Had enough practise? Shall we finish out the night with a sing-a-long?"

Chantelle looked very tired. She yawned and nodded. "It's someone else's turn to sing!"

Daniel's three friends came and sat on the couch. Chantelle snuggled up to Emily, with Mogsy and Rain sleeping on her other side.

"Terry?" Owen asked. "Would you like to play?"

Terry looked shy. But Chantelle's eyes widened.

"Yes! Please, Terry!" she cried.

"Okay," he said, taking over from Owen. "What songs do people want to sing?"

"Something happy," Chantelle said.

"I agree," Emily added with a nod. "And fun to sing. How about *Deck The Halls*?"

"Yeah!" Chantelle cried.

Terry pressed some notes, trying to find the correct key. Then he struck out the beginning chords. Everyone joined in, singing the opening line, followed by an exuberant chorus of *fa la la la la, la la la la!* As the song progressed, their fa la la's became louder, more extravagant and theatrical. By the time the song ended every single person in the room was laughing hysterically, their moods lifted by Christmas cheer.

CHAPTER SIX

There was still snow the next morning, but not enough to keep the school closed. Down in the kitchen at breakfast, Chantelle pouted.

"It's not fair. I don't want to go back to school. I want to build another snow giant."

"Sorry chicken," Emily said, stroking her hair. "But it'll be the Christmas vacation before you know it. And you're probably not going to be doing anything too taxing at this time of year!"

"We all have to go to work anyway," Stu told her, pointing at Clyde and Evan with his thumbs. "So it's not like you're not missing out on anything fun." He winked cheekily.

"And there wouldn't be anyone to help you climb to the top of your ladder," Clyde joined in.

"And," Daniel added, "All your friends will all be at school so you'll have more fun there that you will do here!"

Chantelle seemed cheered up. She looked at Emily. "What are you doing today, mommy?"

Emily took a deep breath. There were two things on her mind she wanted to tackle. The first was calling Vladi. The second was Amy, whom she'd been thinking of ever since their fight. She was always at the back of her mind. She'd been trying to let time heal the rift but perhaps some more action was required on her part. "I've got some calls to make."

"To Vladi?" Chantelle guessed.

Emily nodded. "And Amy. I want to see if she'll meet up with me. We had a bit of a disagreement and I want to patch it up."

Chantelle's eyes widened slightly. "What was the fight about?"

"Grown up stuff. Boring business things."

Chantelle pulled a face. "Oh. Well tell her to stop being silly. It's almost Christmas and you're best friends."

"Wise words," Emily replied.

It was time for Stuart, Evan and Clyde to leave for work, so they stood up then and deposited their dirty crockery in the sink, making their usual clattering noise as they did. Emily sometimes felt like she was living with a herd of elephants having them around the house.

"We'd better get to school, too," Daniel said, looking at the clock. "Ready Chantelle?"

The little girl nodded. She hopped down from her stool and kissed Emily on the cheek, then collected her backpack. Daniel kissed Emily goodbye as well, and she listened as the pair stomped down the hallway and out the front door. With everyone gone, a quietness descended around Emily.

She bit the inside of her mouth as she mulled over the words she would say to Amy on the phone. It seemed as though every time she tried to justify her actions, it upset Amy. So explaining herself would be futile.

She stood and picked up the kitchen phone, a vintage one with a long, curly chord that could stretch all the way to the island. She dialled Vladi's number first.

The call connected a few seconds later. She heard the scritchy voice of Vladi on the other end, answering in Greek.

"Vladi, it's Emily, Roy's daughter."

The elderly man switched straight to English. "Emily, hello! How are you? Has something happened? To the baby?" He sounded panicked, and Emily remembered how she'd promised to only call him in an emergency.

"Nothing's wrong," she assured him. "But to be perfectly honest, I'm worried. Dad isn't replying to my calls or emails."

There was a long pause. Finally Vladi spoke. "I know. I keep telling him he must. But he says no. He needs some space to work something out. That's all he'll say."

"Work something out?" Emily asked. "What does that mean?"

"I don't know, I don't know. But Emily, I think you will just need to be patient. He will call you back in his own time."

Patient? When Roy's time was running out so quickly!

"Can you tell me how he is, at least?" Emily asked. "Is he eating?"

"Oh yes. Like a horse."

"Sailing?"

"Only when the sun is shining. Which is every day."

"Gardening?"

"Morning, noon and night. Truly, Emily, he is quite fine, quite himself. There is just something on his mind that he is processing. My promise still stands good. I will call if there is an emergency. You must trust me."

"I do," Emily said. "I just can't help worrying."

"I understand."

Emily felt greatly reassured by her call with Vladi. Even if it hadn't solved the mystery of why Roy wouldn't speak to her, it was a relief to know he was the same, that his health hadn't deteriorated.

Emily went back to the telephone on the wall. This time she dialled Amy's number before pacing back to one of the stools and sitting.

Amy's caller ID must have shown her who was calling, because she answered with a lacklustre, "Hello."

"Amy, it's me. Look, I know we're never going to agree on certain things, but Chantelle made a great point over breakfast today. It's Christmas. It's time to be together, not fighting. Can we just have a coffee date like normal and chat about everything we usually do and just put that boring business stuff aside. Please?"

She stopped, her prepared monologue over, the ball now in Amy's court.

"Yeah, I guess," Amy replied.

"Really?" Emily said, feeling a heavy weight lift from her chest. "Oh Amy, you have no idea how happy that makes me."

Amy didn't sound as enthused, but her tone brightened a little. "I'm only agreeing to this because I need your help organizing stuff."

"For the wedding?"

"Yes. And the house. And I guess you've done nothing about the babymoon, have you?"

Emily could help but smile to herself. Of course Amy's need to micro-manage everything would be a band aid for the friendship!

"I've got a babysitter," she explained. "But other than that, no. I guess I'm just useless without you."

"Your words not mine," Amy joked, and now she really started to sound like herself again. "Shall I come by yours? I presume I'm driving."

"If you don't mind," Emily replied. The least she could do was give Amy control and let her feel superior. "I hate driving this pregnant."

Amy sighed in that way she did when she was overworked but secretly loving it. "I'll be over in a bit."

Emily stood and placed the telephone's receiver back into the wall bracket. She smiled to herself, relieved to have found a way to fix their issue, even if it was only temporary. She breathed a sigh of relief, relaxing for what felt like the first time in days

Just then, she heard a very soft knocking at the door. Terry poked his head around.

"I'm sorry to disturb you," he said. "I was just wondering if there's anything I could do around the house to help out?"

"There is," Emily said. "You can help out by drinking this coffee and letting me cook you something for breakfast."

Terry blushed. "I can fix myself my own food, Emily. Honestly, you're doing too much for me."

"I just want you to be comfortable here."

"I'd be more comfortable if you gave me chores. Please. I hate to be idle."

Emily considered it. She hated the idea of making her guest work, but Terry clearly needed something to occupy his mind from his troubles.

"Actually, there's a tree at the end of the garden that's going rotten. Perhaps you could cut it down for me?"

She'd never seen someone look so excited by the prospect of chopping down a tree. Terry leapt up immediately.

"I'm on it!"

Emily laughed. "Okay, thank you. But I'll be gone by the time you're done. I'm meeting a friend for a coffee date. Please make yourself comfortable. There might be some staff around, Bryony, I believe will be coming in to work on the website, and Parker's delivering some groceries in about an hour, then he'll be in the kitchen incase we get anyone in for lunch. The restaurant and spa are open so feel free to go to either of them if you get lonely. Oh and Tracey's gentle yoga class is this afternoon if you feel like getting bendy."

"I'll be fine, Emily," Terry assured her. "Don't worry about me."

Emily heard the door open and close, and Amy's voice calling out, "It's me!"

She touched Terry's hand lightly. "Sure you'll be okay?"

He nodded, clearly touched by her generosity. "I will. Thank you."

Emily stood and went to find Amy.

She was in the foyer, waiting, in extremely unpractical heeled boots.

"You do know it's icy today?" Emily laughed, eyeing them. She slipped on her own flat, comfy, wooly ones.

She was just about to follow Amy out to the car when the phone started to ring. Bryony hadn't arrived yet to cover the phones so Emily picked up the call, using her hostess voice. To her surprise it was Daniel on the other end.

"Guess what? Jack's given me an extra day off. He told his wife that I'd been snowed in today and had to cover my shift because he really wants to work on this fairytale treehouse castle order that's come in for a Christmas gift."

"Oh," Emily laughed. "Jack is terrible. He really needs to be honest about not wanting to retire. He's going to get you in trouble."

"I don't mind," Daniel replied. "It means I can come and spend the day with my beautiful wife."

"But I have plans with Amy," Emily told him. "We're doing the triple organization today -- wedding, house, babymoon."

"Think she'd want to make it quadruple?" Daniel asked.

"I don't understand," Emily said, frowning.

She could hear the grin in Daniel's voice as he replied. "The woodshop. *My* woodshop."

"You told Jack you're starting your own store?" she exclaimed, feeling excitement ripple through her. "What did he say?"

"He's really happy for me," Daniel said. "So what do you think? Shall we look for shop locations?"

Emily looked up at Amy. "How do you feel about Daniel coming along today and scouting a spot for his shop?" she asked.

"How do I feel about it?" Amy asked, her eyes widening with glee. "I feel fantastic about it! Four things to plan in one day? Bring it on."

Emily spoke back into the phone. "We have a resounding yes from Amy. Meet you in town?"

"Great," Daniel replied. "See you there!"

*

Emily sat in the back of Amy's car with babymoon brochures spread all over the back seats. Daniel was in the passenger seat with a cellphone latched to his ear, speaking to the real estate agent about a shop location. Amy, meanwhile, was driving whilst on speaker phone to a wedding venue.

"I'd love to book a viewing with you today," Emily heard her say. "I'm on a tight schedule, though. Are you free at one?"

Emily reached for the notebook where she'd been writing their itinerary. "Amy, we're seeing a house at one. Make it one thirty."

"Sorry," Amy called into the speaker. "One thirty?"

"We can do one thirty," the voice crackled back.

"Fab," Amy said. "See you then." She ended the call and spoke over her shoulder. "Got that, Em?"

Emily quickly scrawled the meeting down, squeezing it in between two other appointments. "Got it." Then she grabbed the brochure from her lap and handed it to Daniel. "This is the place. I'm certain. What do you think?"

She'd selected the place in Quebec that Amy had first mentioned to her. Of all the packages offered, it looked like the best value for money and the location was phenomenal, not to mention the fact the actual building looked like a miniature castle!

With the cellphone resting between his ear and shoulder, Daniel's eyes scanned the double page spread. "Great, two p.m. is perfect," he said aloud into the phone. Then he nodded at Emily, indicating his agreement at her choice of venue.

She took the brochure back and called the number.

"I'd like to book your babymoon package for next weekend," she said when the call connected.

"I'm afraid we're fully booked for next weekend," the woman on the phone replied. "But I've just had a cancellation for tomorrow and Sunday. Could you make that?"

"Tomorrow?" Emily cried. She leaned forward and tapped Daniel. But he was in mid conversation. She spoke again into the phone. "I'd have to check with my husband. Can I call you back?"

"You can," the woman said. "But I honestly think it will go soon. It's not often we get last minute spaces like this."

Emily chewed her lip in deliberation. She knew Yvonne wouldn't mind the last minute change. And Daniel had seemed uncharacteristically relaxed about the idea of a weekend away.

"Just book it," Amy told her from the driver's seat.

"Okay," Emily said. "We'll take it."

She gave her details and payment information to the woman and ended the call. Amy was looking at her in the rear view mirror.

"That was lucky!" Emily said. "They were fully booked but had had a last minute cancellation."

"This weekend is better anyway," Amy told her. "Baby Charlotte might be here by next weekend!"

Emily touched her stomach. There was no way of knowing. Half of the people she met seemed to think the baby would be early, others seemed dead certain she'd be a Christmas baby. Emily just wanted her to do whatever she wanted, to trust nature and fate to give her a safe delivery and a happy, healthy newborn.

Daniel finished his call to the real estate agent. "Can you put down a three p.m. meeting for me?" he asked, turning to look at Emily in the back seat.

She added it to their list of meetings. When she was finished writing, she looked back at Daniel.

"Hon, I booked the babymoon."

"You did?" he replied. "But why do you look so worried?"

Emily bit her lip. "Because we're going tomorrow."

Daniel laughed heartily. "That's fine by me," he said. "After the day we're about to have, we're going to need it!"

Emily laughed too and looked at her list. They had a jam-packed schedule.

"I feel like I'm back at work in New York," she said.

"Blame me," Amy replied. "As they say, you can take the girl out of New York…"

She pulled up then outside the wedding venue they were to see first. Unlike Emily's choices when she'd been scouring the local area for quaint, historic buildings to marry in, Amy's tastes were quite the opposite. She liked sleek, modern buildings, grand and luxurious. This one ticked all the boxes, at least from the outside.

"This is what Raven's inn will be like," Amy told her as she climbed out the car.

Emily looked up at the tall, glass building and grimaced. It would be such an eyesore in Sunset Harbor. Completely ill fitting with the rest of the town. Maybe she should have opposed the plan after all.

"Are you sure?" Emily said hopefully. "You don't think she'd tone it down a bit?"

"Why would she?" Amy replied, a little haughtily. "Because Sunset Harbor is more special than all the other towns she's ruined? She's not going to waste money on new architect plans or meetings with the builders. She's just going to plonk a carbon copy of all her other places in the gap. And that's what it will be like."

Emily bit her lip, feeling worse than ever. She needed to speak to Raven, business woman to business woman, and make her see sense. She'd be reviled in the town if she built a monstrosity like this on the oceanfront!

They went inside to look at the venue and Amy seemed very pleased. It was clean, bright and modern, with a glitzy restaurant area and a large outside greenhouse-like building where the weddings took place.

"Yes, this is quite lovely," Amy said, looking around with her nose in the air, as if she could sniff out cheapness.

"Don't you need to check with Harry first?" Emily asked.

Amy rolled her eyes. "Are you joking? Harry would get married in a log cabin if I let him have any say! He's not got the

61

best taste in the world. We've already sorted it all out. I'll be organizing everything. All he has to do is turn up."

Everyone laughed.

Amy spoke then to the guide, telling her that she'd be in touch but so far they were the top of her list. Then she, Daniel and Emily hurried off, heading back to the car and their next meeting.

"Where are we going?" Amy asked Emily.

"Shop visit," Emily said, reading from the list. "Chestnut drive."

"I'm on it," Amy said.

She revved the engine and they spend off.

The drive from the wedding venue wasn't long, but from Sunset Harbor it would be close to forty five minutes.

"Do you really want to be commuting so far each day?" Emily asked Daniel as they got out the car.

He shook his head. "Probably not. I mean one of the reasons Jack's been so successful is that he was always there to pull an all nighter if needed. I want to be able to do that if I need to."

The store was very cute, but the attached woodworking shop was on the small side, and besides, the town it was in wasn't particularly large.

"I think I'd prefer somewhere in Sunset Harbor," Daniel said. "Close to home. Close to friends."

"Let's hope your three p.m. is the one then," Emily said.

Their next three meetings took them back towards Sunset Harbor. First there was a house that Amy didn't like, then a wedding venue that Amy didn't like, and finally another house that Amy didn't like. As the afternoon fell, they were right back into Sunset Harbor for the final two meetings.

"Okay," Amy said, turning them down a single track road in the hills. "This is the last house of the day."

"It's quite close to us," Emily noted, looking down through the thicket of trees to the ocean, knowing their own home was in that general direction. "I bet there's a shortcut through the trees."

Daniel spoke then. "I think it's parallel to us, actually. We must be just there, the other side of those woods."

"You're right," Amy said. "I can see your widow's walk."

"Oh yes!" Emily cried. "I hope this is the one. Can you imagine if we just had to walk through a forest to visit each other?"

"Sounds ideal," Amy agreed.

The path grew even narrower and the trees darker. It was a bit spooky, but Emily didn't say anything because she didn't want to put Amy off.

Finally, they pulled up outside the large family home. It had a curved, paved driveway, and neatly trimmed hedges. The house looked extremely well cared for. There was a porch with carved wooden columns, a glass door with gold numbers screwed on, and a large garage to one side.

"Um…" Emily began. "This is gorgeous."

"Let's wait until we're inside," Amy said. But Emily could hear the trembling excitement in her voice.

The agent was waiting in the driveway. He was a young man with a wide grin. He didn't look much older than twenty-four.

"Max Ngyung," he said, holding out his hand to shake everyone's. "Which one of you is Amy?"

"The would be me," Amy said, shaking his hand back.

"I'm so excited to show you this property," the young man told them. "We've been working on it for the last few months."

"Oh?" Amy asked, curious.

"Yeah I have a business with my brothers. We buy local properties, do them up so they're modern and luxurious, and sell them on to lovely people like yourself. This is our third house."

Amy seemed impressed. Emily certainly was. For a young man, Max had made a great success of himself.

"How did you get into this line of work?" Emily asked.

"Long story," he told her. "My parents came over from Vietnam. They had a restaurant when I was a kid, down in Portland. Great place. Proper home cooked Vietnamese food. We all chipped in when we were old enough, washing dishes, waiting tables, delivering take out on our bikes! We were always supposed to follow in their footsteps and take over the restaurant when they retired. But then my dad died suddenly. We got a bit of insurance money through and Mom didn't want to stop running the restaurant, so she gave it to us to start our own business, anything we wanted. We went for property development."

"That's great," Daniel told him. "It looks like you have a real flair for it."

Max's enthusiasm for the property was infectious.

"Okay, this living room is awesome," he said. "Walnut wood floors. Cream walls. All fresh plastering. This fireplace works, we had the chimney's unblocked and cleaned because who doesn't want a proper fire for Christmas and Thanksgiving? Over here we have the dining room area which would be an awesome place for hosting events. You see this wall folds back so you can join the two rooms together." He demonstrated by pulling the screen back. Then he pointed up. "Chandelier. But watch this." He twisted a dimmer switch. "Romance." Then he twisted it all the way up. "Party!"

Emily laughed. Max wasn't even a salesman, he just took so much pride in his work it sold itself. She could tell as they walked through that Amy had fallen instantly in love with the place. She was trying to keep it in but a smile kept bursting through her lips when she thought no one was looking.

Max showed them the kitchen complete with an enormous fridge and all the modcons.

"The coffee machine comes with the house?" Amy asked.

"Yeah, it's our thing," he said, chuckling. "Coffee machine with every purchase. You drink coffee?"

"Of course," Amy replied, smiling.

Upstairs there were three bedrooms -- a master with an en suite and two generously sized rooms -- as well as a family bathroom and study that was down its own corridor with a door separating it from the rest.

"I work from home so this would be great," she said. "It's far enough away to feel like a separate space."

"I work from home too," Max said. "That's why we made it that way. With the kids and pets running around, you need somewhere that's just a little bit away from all the noise. Do you have kids?"

"Not yet," Amy said.

She didn't say it aloud, but Emily could hear in her tone the implied *soon*.

"Shall I let you guys look around by yourselves?" Max asked. "Or we could book another day for you to see it. Give you time to think it through. Let it sink in."

"Yes, that would be great," Amy said.

They all went back out to the driveway and shook Max's hand, then got back into Amy's car.

"Oh my God that house," Amy gushed. "And the real estate agent was such a cutey!"

"You can tell he's really passionate about his work," Emily agreed. "I think you'd be a fool to miss out on this opportunity. The house is in great shape. He's thought everything through in terms of what a young, modern family would want out of their property. Plus they're a small, local business and there's no chain. It's basically perfect."

"It is," Amy agreed.

"And we're five minutes away," Daniel added.

"I'll get Harry to come and see it tomorrow," Amy told them both. "I'm sure he'll love it too."

"Will you put an offer in?" Emily asked, excitement mounting in her.

Amy nodded, a little smirk on her lips.

"YAY!" Emily cried, sounding just like Chantelle on snow day.

"We'd better hurry to the harbor," Daniel said. "My store appointment is in five minutes."

Amy stepped on it, and the car careened down the hills towards the ocean front. The store was on a side road round the edge of the harbor, so a little off the beaten track. But it was in a bustling area and people walked along with their arms laden with shopping bags.

Amy parked up beside the sidewalk.

"It looks cute," Emily said, looking out the window at the small store squished between a hardware store and vintage clothing shop. "What do you think, Daniel?"

"I like the location," he said. "But isn't it a bit on the small side?"

They got out the car and went into the store. It was set over two floors, with a lovely wooden staircase in the middle. The store, though narrow, stretched back farther than expected, and with the extra floor it was quite a considerable space.

They climbed the steps and saw that on the top floor, the ceiling was peaked, making it feel like an attic room. One wall was all glass, and the view was onto the ocean.

"I bet on a clear day you can see our island," Daniel said.

They went back down the steps and out through the door at the back, which led to the woodshop area. It was much larger than Emily had anticipated, and would easily fit in the heavy duty equipment Daniel would need to install.

"Maybe I'm being a bit rash," Daniel said. "But I'm getting a really good vibe about this place. Would it be mad to make an offer?"

Emily raised her eyebrows. "If you do, it will be four for four, right? Babymoon booked, wedding venue located, Amy's house found, it's the last thing. Fate has been good to us today. So maybe it's a sign."

"It's a ten minute drive to the house. Close to Chantelle's school. I mean, when she's a little older she'll be able to drop by after school, then we can take the boat out together."

He looked dreamy, like he was looking forward to an idyllic future he'd not envisaged until this moment.

"Daniel," Emily said, taking his hands. "I think this is it. This is your shop."

"I think so too," he said.

And with that, their busy day of organization came to an end, with every single thing ticked off their list. There'd been not a single compromise to make. They'd each gotten exactly what they wanted. And, even better, they had an amazing babymoon planned for the next day! It really could not have gone better, Emily thought. She sat in the back seat of Amy's car, excited, and filled with anticipation for the babymoon, and all the exciting changes to come.

CHAPTER SEVEN

The drive to the spa in Quebec was to take just over five hours, so Emily set her alarm to wake her up at six a.m. Saturday morning. She wanted them to get an early start on the roads to try and beat the traffic.

Her alarm beeped loudly and Emily turned over in bed to stop it. Then she shook Daniel gently awake.

"Are you ready for our babymoon?" she asked him.

He smiled through his evident sleepiness.

They both washed and dressed for the day, and carried their cases down to the car. It was freezing outside, with frost glittering on the surface of the car as well as the grass. Emily loved frost, it was like everything had been covered in diamonds. Once the sun rose, it would be a real sight to behold.

With everything ready, they crept quietly into Chantelle's room. It was still dark, and the only sound was the child's soft snoring.

"Honey," Daniel whispered, crouching next to her. "We're leaving now. We'll be back Sunday evening."

Chantelle made a grumpy murmuring sort of sound. Daniel moved away and Emily leant down, kissing her on the forehead.

"Have the best time at Bailey's," she whispered.

Chantelle snored in reply.

Daniel and Emily headed back downstairs.

"Can you smell coffee?" Emily asked, frowning.

It wouldn't be unusual for the breakfast shift to begin this early usually, but there were no guests at the moment and therefore no one to make coffee for. Evan, Stu and Clyde were taking the day off as well.

"I do," Daniel said.

They went down the hall to the kitchen to see what was going on and were surprised to see Terry awake.

"Good morning," Emily said. "We didn't wake you, did we?"

Terry shook his head. "No, I wanted to make sure you had some breakfast before you left for Quebec. I made oatmeal and raisin bars. And here's some coffee."

He handed them a thermos. Emily took it, surprised.

"You didn't have to do that!" she said, touched by the gesture.

"It's the least I can do," he said. "And you know how I feel about idle hands! I don't suppose you have any more trees that need felling?"

Emily shook her head. "Just the rotten one you took down for us yesterday."

But Daniel raised his eyebrows suddenly. "You know there are some trees that need to be pulled down on the island. I'm not sure if the weather will be good enough today, but it's forecast to be clear tomorrow. If you want you can head over with the guys. They'll show you what needs doing."

Emily worried that he'd feel taken advantage of, but instead Terry looked utterly thrilled.

"Oh thank you," he gushed, shaking Daniel's hands. "That would be wonderful."

"No, thank you," Daniel replied. "The quicker we get the work there done the better. Anyway, we ought to leave or we'll be late. Thanks for the breakfast!"

They said farewell to Terry then headed out the kitchen and into the foyer. Marnie was on the desk today, using the quietness to do school work behind the counter. She was on 'Chantelle Watch' until Yvonne came to pick her up, but hopefully she would just sleep straight through.

"Have the best time," Marnie told them, waving goodbye.

There was still no sign of the sunrise as they walked down the porch steps and got into the pickup truck.

"Ready?" Daniel asked, leaning over and resting his hand on Emily's.

"Ready," she grinned back.

He started the car, revved the engine, and they were off.

*

Thanks to the breakfast bars Terry had provided them with, the journey wasn't anywhere as tiring as Emily had expected it to be. Waking up so early was something she'd done at the beginning of the business, but these days, in the third trimester, Emily usually stayed in bed as long as possible. She'd thought the journey would exhaust her and was pleasantly surprised with how awake she felt as they pulled up outside the castle-style spa, which was situated on the outskirts of Quebec City.

Daniel whistled loudly. "Looks even better in real life," he said.

"Amy has a great eye for taste," Emily agreed.

The small castle was built on the hillsides, with an amazing stone walkway that zigzagged upwards through shrubbery and hedgerows, leading up to a huge arched door that wouldn't look out of place in a cathedral. There were even turrets!

Daniel carried their cases up the slope and Emily walked slowly beside him, her hands on her stomach. Then they reached the large door and pushed it open.

Inside, it no longer felt like they were in a castle. Instead, the floor was shiny white tiles, like those in their own spa, and there were Edison light bulbs on ropes hanging down from the ceiling. Glass vases filled with lavender were positioned all around the room, and there was a large white leather couch, glass shelves displaying products like shampoo and moisturizing cream. The whole space was very bright, clean and fresh. Soft piano music played in the background.

They approached the frosted glass counter, where a young woman dressed in a white uniform was smiling at them.

"Bonjour," she said. "Good day."

"We have a booking under the name Morey," Daniel told her.

The woman typed into her computer. "The two-day, one-night babymoon package," she confirmed. She went over to a cabinet and took out a key. "You're in room three."

Daniel took the key and thanked her, then they walked through the pristine hallways towards the elevator.

Their room was on the next floor up. Daniel used the key to open up the door, and they walked into the gorgeous, bright room. It was exquisitely decorated in gold and white, with sweeping lace curtains framing floor to ceiling windows. On the bed there was a large basket with a white ribbon tied on the handle.

"What's this?" Emily squealed, hurrying over to look inside. "Baby things!"

Inside was the softest white blanket, a pair to white booties for a newborn, a pack of three white, simple babygrows, and the most adorable mobile which was designed like a fluffy cloud with stars and birds coming from it.

"How wonderful," Emily gushed.

Daniel sat down onto the bed and picked up the treatment itinerary on the pillow. He began to read.

"For mom-to-be, please enjoy an algae body wrap, prenatal massage, and facial treatment. Dad-to-be can enjoy our sauna and stress-busting deep tissue massage. Green cleanse juices are available from reception." He wiggled his eyebrows at Emily. "What do think? Green juice?"

She rubbed her stomach. "I'd prefer some lunch. What's on the menu?" She found the menu on the bedside table. "Avocado and arugula salad served on sourdough bread with homemade hummus and tomatoes grown in our own greenhouse. Well that sounds delightful."

"Let's eat!" Daniel exclaimed. "I've had nothing but Terry's oatmeal bar."

They locked up their room and went down to the dining room. Like the rest of the hotel, it was decorated with frosted glass, white tiles, exposed brick and Edison bulbs. It really was gorgeous.

They took a table.

"Daniel," Emily whispered, leaning across. "I'm by far the most pregnant person here."

"We did leave it quite late," he laughed, looking around at all the women with their small, neat bumps.

Their food came and they enjoyed the fresh, healthy lunch, ordering green juices to wash it all down. Daniel went for cucumber and spinach with pear, whilst Emily had aojiru, which was a Japanese kale based cleanser.

Once they'd eaten, it was time for their first pamper session. They headed to the couple treatment rooms, pleased to see they wouldn't be separated during their respective treatments.

Emily found her massage very relaxing. So much so she could easily have drifted off to sleep, had it not been for Daniel's occasional grunts and groans during his more vigorous deep-tissue massage. After, they went to the heated pool to enjoy a gentle swim.

"Would you like to have dinner here?" Daniel asked Emily. "Or would you prefer to spend the evening in Quebec City?"

"I'd like to dine out," Emily said. "And see some of the city. It would be a shame not to. Who knows when we'll next get the chance."

They went up to their room to wash from the swim and dress up for a meal out. Emily didn't have many fancy maternity clothes, but she did have a nice, simple black dress that she accentuated with delicate gold jewelry. Daniel didn't really do formal attire, but he'd brought a nice clean plaid shirt and changed into black jeans and leather shoes.

"You look very handsome," Emily told him.

"And you look stunningly beautiful," Daniel replied.

They kissed. Then, hand in hand, they walked out the bedroom, locking it behind them. They took the elevator down to the reception area, then stepped outside. To Emily's great delight, it was snowing.

"How wonderful," she murmured.

They strolled slowly, taking in the sights as they went, of Old Quebec City decorated for Christmas. There were fairy lights in all the tree branches, and glittery model snowflakes hung across the road, strung between the telephone poles either side of the street. Street lamps caught the falling snowflakes, making them look like small fluttering lights. Emily found it utterly charming. They passed the walls of the Citadel, which looked magnificent and very grand in the falling snow.

"This is a beautiful city, isn't it?" Emily murmured to Daniel.

"Beautiful city, beautiful wife. I'd say I'm one lucky guy."

"And I'm one lucky gal," she giggled in response.

He squeezed her hand tenderly and Emily felt more in love than ever. How wonderful life could be, she thought.

They reached the restaurant and went inside. It was a gorgeous, intimate place, decorated like a vintage tea room.

"Oh I just love it!" Emily gushed, looking at all the cute, unique, vintage pieces of furniture. "Do you remember when we'd go antique shopping every weekend?" she asked Daniel.

He took his seat opposite her. "Yes. And look how far we've come. Back then it was just you and I, with a dilapidated inn. Now we have Chantelle, a gorgeous home, dogs and chickens and the thriving business."

"And an island," Emily prompted.

"How many people can say that!" Daniel chuckled.

"We've been blessed."

"We have. And the blessings are going to keep coming, once Charlotte comes."

Emily smiled and rubbed her stomach tenderly. Then she turned her attention to the menu.

"What are you eating?" she asked. "I might go for the meatball ragout."

"I'm getting the poutine of course!" Daniel exclaimed. "I've been running on oatmeal, avocado and cucumber all day. I need some fries and cheese!"

Emily giggled. She felt suddenly very young, like she had stepped back in time to two-years hence, when they'd been dating and first falling in love. They had come so far, achieved so much, and her love for Daniel had only deepened. But it was easy to get caught up in life, to become so busy they forgot to express their love and appreciation. She reached across the table and took Daniel's hands, and looked dreamily into his eyes.

"You're the best thing that's ever happened to me," she said.

"I am?" Daniel asked. "Not the inn?"

"There would be no inn without you," she told him. "I'd never have gotten so far without your support and hard work and dedication. The inn may have brought me to Maine in the first place, but you're the reason I stayed."

Daniel's eyes looked misty, like he might be holding back tears. Emily was surprised to see the sudden display of emotion from him.

"I don't deserve you," he said. "I never knew I could have a life like this. I'd never have believed it if you'd told me back when I was sixteen that I'd have all this to look forward to! Sometimes I have to pinch myself."

Emily squeezed his hands, trying to communicate her love and appreciation through the gesture. She'd not felt such burning love from Daniel since that moment they'd said their vows.

"I love you," she told him. "For now and forever."

"I love you," he said. "Forever and always."

CHAPTER EIGHT

TWO WEEKS LATER

Emily's due date -- December 13th -- came and went with no sign of Baby Charlotte. At 40 weeks pregnant, she was bigger than ever, but not uncomfortable in the way she'd been expecting. She didn't feel any sense of urgency to get the pregnancy over and done with. In fact, she was feeling healthier now than she had any point thus far.

"We should book an appointment with Doctor Arkwright," Daniel said over breakfast.

"She's only a few days overdue," Emily said. "If there's no sign of her by the 20th, we'll go then. Then I'll be a week overdue and we can think about what to do."

"Okay," he said, sounding a bit weary.

Emily didn't mind. It was his job to worry. But she knew her body and knew that everything was fine.

Chantelle looked up from her clock. "What do you mean about what to do?"

"There's a few things they can do to try and make the labour start," Emily explained. "I'd like to avoid them all if possible."

"Are they dangerous?" the child asked. She looked concerned.

"Not at all," Emily reassured her. "I just want to trust my body. It knows what it wants to do."

Chantelle looked calmed. She went back to her clock.

Daniel, on the other hand, did not. It seemed that the longer Emily remained pregnant, the more stressed he became. She could appreciate that there was a thin line between anticipation and anxiety, but surely if anyone should be anxious it should be her! She was the one who'd be doing all the pushing, and the longer Charlotte stayed inside the bigger she became!

"What are your Hanukkah plans?" Emily asked Daniel, changing the subject. "It starts tonight, doesn't it?"

"Chantelle and I will light the menorah," he said. "And read some scripture."

"What about Roman's party?" Chantelle asked, looking up again with big, concerned eyes. "We can't miss it! It's going to be amazing!"

Daniel frowned. His mood seemed to be growing darker. "Darling, our traditions are important, too. Roman should have chosen a different date, to be respectful."

Emily patted his arm. "Roman's hosting an event for the whole town and we should be grateful," she warned him. "And Chantelle, we won't miss any of the party, but remember that Hanukkah is very important to daddy, and it means a lot to him to teach you about it."

Chantelle nodded, looking humbled and put in her place. Emily felt satisfied to have resolved the situation. Even Daniel's mood seemed to brighten after that.

"Time for school," he said to Chantelle, standing. He went over and kissed Emily on the head. "Call me if you need to," he said. He'd been saying the same thing every day since her due date, as if he was worried Emily would go into labour but decide not to disturb him! She was not prepared to give birth on the inn floor!

They went out into the corridor, and Emily heard Daniel call up to Terry, who was coming to the island today to do some more landscaping work. As soon as everyone was gone, Emily soaked in the silence. She enjoyed these moments the most, when it was just her and Baby Charlotte, and the ever present spirit of her sister, guiding her, supporting her, loving her.

*

That evening, Roman was hosting his holiday cocktail party. The family got themselves dressed up in their smartest outfits, and Emily plaited Chantelle's hair in an intricate style. When Evan, Stu and Clyde came down the stairs, Emily exclaimed in delight.

"Look at you three!"

She'd not seen them look so smart since the wedding!

"Where's Terry?" Chantelle asked, when it was just about time to leave.

"I don't know," Emily replied. "Why don't you go and knock on his door and see if he's ready."

Chantelle nodded, and hurried off, her elegant dress in no way hampering her boisterousness. Terry had taken the smallest room on the third floor, even though Emily had assured him that he didn't have to hide himself away. But he'd insisted he was used to a smaller room and it made him feel more at home.

Chantelle reappeared at the top of the flight of stairs.

"He says he didn't know he was invited."

"Oh," Emily said sadly. Roman's cocktail party was an event for the whole of Sunset Harbor, but Terry was from out of town so probably hadn't realized. "Is he coming now?"

Chantelle thunked down the staircase. "He says he hasn't got anything nice to wear."

Emily cast an appealing gaze at Daniel. "Can you lend him something? It wouldn't be right to leave him here on his own when the whole town is celebrating."

Daniel nodded and went upstairs to fetch some clothes. After a few minutes, he and Terry appeared. Terry looked uncomfortable in one of Daniel's ever-so-slightly too tight shirts.

Chantelle started clapping. "Oh, Uncle Terry, you look awesome!"

The nickname was clearly not lost on Terry. He smiled widely, looking extremely touched.

At last everyone was ready, and they headed out the inn. The family climbed into Daniel's truck whilst everyone else got into Clyde's, then they drove the short distance through town to Roman's mansion.

The roof was decorated with a million white fairy lights, and all along the driveway there were small lanterns with candles burning inside of them. There were also a row of winter trees, sprayed with fake snow and sparkling silver glitter.

"This is so beautiful," Chantelle gasped.

It was still quite early but the house was already buzzing with activity. From inside, Christmas jazz music emanated. Everyone headed eagerly inside.

Inside, the mansion was decorated just as impeccably, carrying the silver and white lights theme of the outside in. There was a long silver carpet stretching along the corridor, leading them to the kitchen-dining room area where the party was being held. They followed the carpet, feeling like film stars.

They walked into the kitchen and saw that the room looked like winter wonderland. Huge metallic white balloons floated in all four corners of the room. Delicate glass snowflakes and icicles were strung in chains across the ceiling, twinkling as they caught the light coming from the myriad of lanterns and candelabras. It was so stunning.

"Isn't it fantastic?" Emily gushed to Chantelle.

The child looked awed.

Straight away, Chantelle spotted some of her school friends and ran off to play with them. Stu, Evan and Clyde headed immediately towards the alcohol stand. Once they reached it, they turned and beckoned Daniel over.

"Free bar!" Stu cried across the room.

Daniel turned a deep shade of red in his embarrassment. Emily chuckled.

"Well go on then," she urged him.

He scurried after his friends, leaving Emily with just Terry.

She turned to face him. "Let me introduce you to Roman."

They wended through the groups of people to where Roman was chatting in the corner with some of his management staff; fashionably dressed men and woman whom she occasionally saw wandering around town looking very out of place.

"Emily!" Roman said, waving as she approached. "Still pregnant, I see."

"Four days overdue and counting," Emily said with a nod, rubbing her stomach.

"Well if you go into labor tonight, don't panic. Sofia here is a doula." He patted the shoulder of one of his entourage, a hippy looking girl covered in beaded jewellry and bangles, who reminded Emily of Bryony.

"I don't think she has any plans on coming soon," Emily told him with a chuckle. She gestured to the room. "It looks fab this year. A real winter wonderland."

"I can't take credit for it," Roman said. "I have Gretta to thank for the design."

He gestured to a woman in the group, who was wearing a barely-there gold dress, strappy heels and matching jewellry. Her rouge-painted lips twitched into an imperceptible smile.

"I wanted to introduce you to Terry," Emily said. "He's our guest at the inn this Christmas."

Roman shook his hand warmly. "You're the fellow who owned the Christmas tree farm, aren't you? I heard about the fire. You have my deepest sympathy."

"Thank you," Terry said, his eyes dropping to the floor.

Emily felt terrible for him. Every time his farm was mentioned, it seemed to cause him a fresh wave of grief, like a scab being constantly ripped off.

"Terry's been delighting us with his hidden talent," Emily told Roman, trying to steer the conversation to something happier. "Singing and playing the piano."

"Another musician!" Roman beamed. "You'll have to try out my studio. I've had the Sunset Harbor kids record a choir part for my Christmas charity single. Perhaps you'd like to add some piano to it?"

Terry's eyes widened. "That would be wonderful."

"Fantastic. We're laying down some tracks tomorrow morning. Can you come by with Chantelle?"

Terry looked at Emily, stunned. "Is that okay?"

Emily wiggled her eyebrows at him. "Of course! I bet you're glad you came now," she said.

"Great, it's a date," Roman said. Before anyone had a chance to reply, his attention was distracted by two people entering into the room. "Astrid! George!"

Emily felt an instant cold chill overcome her. She looked over to where Daniel's gorgeous ex girlfriend sashayed in wearing a gorgeous outfit that showed off her amazingly honed body. Her arm was linked with George, Harry's handsome older brother. Thanks to some string pulling from Daniel, Astrid's life had suddenly clicked into place. She'd been hired as Roman's personal assistant and found herself a gorgeous boyfriend. Emily watched on, filled with petty jealousy, as Astrid air-kissed Roman's fashionable entourage. Unlike Emily she fit right in with them all. Emily couldn't help feeling suddenly frumpy and out of place.

Just then the song over the stereo changed to a Christmas pop classic.

"Let's dance!" Roman cried from the other side of the room.

He herded his gang of beautiful, successful young things to the dance floor. Emily hung back, not wanting to be under the spotlights. She watched on from the sidelines, berating her childish feelings of envy.

"Come on everyone!" Roman cried.

More people joined him under the flashing lights. Emily saw Stu, Evan and Clyde jostling Daniel over to the dancing area, and as if in horrible slow motion, she saw the moment come when they bumped into Astrid. Her stomach clenched as the five childhood friends let out cries of delight, hugging each other with the unbridled joy of long lost friends reunited. Just like he did with Chantelle, Clyde heaved Astrid up onto his shoulder and paraded her around as she squealed and kicked. Emily averted her eyes, feeling stupid.

"Emily, are you okay?" she heard a voice say from beside her. It sounded just like Roy. But when she turned, it was Terry standing there.

"I just don't feel like dancing," she said, brushing off her feelings. "And I can't enjoy the cocktails either."

He chuckled. "I must admit I feel like quite the old fogey amongst all these people."

"Not at all!" Emily exclaimed. "Roman's parties are for everyone. There are plenty of Sunset Harbor's more mature folk here. Look." She pointed through the crowds. "There's Derek Hansen!"

The mayor was dancing with abandon, showing off some extremely embarrassing moves.

"And there's Cynthia," she added, pointing at her eccentric neon orange-haired friend. She was wearing a dress that had a huge satin bow on the front. With a chuckle, Emily added, "Dressed to impress, I see."

Looking around the crowds, Emily realized how silly she'd been being. Her heart was full of joy thanks to the wonderful people of Sunset Harbor, the happy kids, the merry parents, the carefree elders. Who cared about her big baby bump, or the extra pounds she'd gained during pregnancy. Tonight was about celebrating. About dancing and singing.

She grabbed Terry's hand.

"Come on. Let's join in."

He resisted at first, shaking his head and turning pink. "Oh I couldn't. I can't dance."

"Me neither," Emily told him, and she urged him into the crowd with her. "No one's watching. Just throw your arms in the air and enjoy yourself."

She finally followed her own advice, letting her hair down, allowing her silly insecurities to fall away. Terry copied her, and soon they were dancing together like crazy people.

Suddenly, she noticed people all around her, joining in with her and Terry's wacky dance moves. Daniel and Evan, then Stu, Clyde and Chantelle.

Just then Roman appeared and gave Chantelle a big cuddle. Emily giggled, delighted to see Chantelle so happy.

"How is my favorite little singer?" Roman asked her, taking her hands to dance. "Will you sing us a song tonight?"

Chantelle blushed. "I might. But only if you sing with me."

Emily watched on as Roman twirled Chantelle on the spot. "Of course! My whole band is here. We'll all perform together."

"Speaking of performances," Emily said. "Chantelle's school one is tomorrow."

"A Seussified Christmas Carol," Chantelle told him, shouting to be heard over the music.

"I love Doctor Seuss," Roman grinned. "Who are you playing?"

"The Ghost of Christmas Past."

"So the best role," Roman said with a nod. "I'd expect no less."

"Scrooge is the biggest part," Chantelle said, shaking her head.

"Maybe," Roman replied. "But no one wants to be the bad guy! You're much better off as the Ghost."

"Can you come?" Chantelle asked, blinking up at Roman with her innocent blue eyes.

"Oh honey," Roman said, suddenly sounding concerned. "I'm so sorry but I can't. I'm out of town all day tomorrow. Morning TV shows." He made a theatrical yawn gesture.

"That's okay," Chantelle replied, her voice heavy with disappointment. "Papa Roy and Nana Patty are going to miss it too."

Emily felt a tug at her heartstrings. This was Chantelle's big moment and so many people she cared about wouldn't be there to see it.

"Tell you what," Roman told her, clearly picking up on her sadness. "If your mommy and daddy film it for me, we can sit down together in my home cinema, eat some popcorn, and have a big screening of your show. What do you say to that?"

Chantelle grinned widely. She had only one thing to that, and it made Emily and Roman both laugh heartily; "Coooool."

CHAPTER NINE

The next evening, Emily was extremely excited as she readied herself to go and see Chantelle's play. Like the rest of her grade, the girl had stayed behind after school for the dress rehearsal, and now the time had arrived for the parents to head over to the school and take their seats in the hall.

As she slicked on some lipstick in the mirror, Emily spoke to her bump. "No surprises tonight, please. This is Chantelle's big day."

Imagine if the baby decided to arrive today, right in the middle of Chantelle's solo!

"You're five days overdue, what's another going to matter?"

Emily laughed then, realizing she was trying to reason with her unborn child. She stood back from the vanity table and observed herself in the floor length mirror beside it. In the figure-hugging dress she'd chosen for the evening, she looked enormous! If she had to guess, she'd think she were carrying twins by the size of her!

She heard the front door slam. Daniel, home from work.

"Are you ready, love?" he called up the staircase.

Emily left her bedroom. "I'm ready," she said.

She made it to the top step. Daniel, who had been fiddling with his phone, glanced up at her.

"WOW!" he exclaimed. "You look stunning, my love."

"Why thank you," Emily replied coyly, taking careful steps down the long flight of stairs. "I thought I looked like a whale personally."

She reached the bottom and Daniel enveloped her in his arms. "You look gorgeous."

She took her coat from the hook by the door and slipped it on, then Daniel put a protective arm around her shoulder as he led her out to the car.

"There's frost on the steps," he said. "Be careful."

It was very dark out, and the air was freezing. "We might be in for more snow soon," Emily commented.

"I hope not," Daniel said. "I'd like to have clear roads to drive you to hospital when the time comes."

"If it ever comes," Emily joked.

They reached the car and Daniel opened the passenger door for her. She had to admit, she was loving this extremely chivalrous version of Daniel that had appeared once she'd gone over her due date!

"How are you feeling?" Daniel asked once she was safely in her seat. "Any hints that labor might be coming?"

He clipped her seatbelt in, as Emily shook her head. "None at all. She's very active at the moment, like she's gearing herself up. But she doesn't feel ready."

Daniel went around to his side of the car. "When are we seeing Doctor Arkwright next?" he asked.

"Monday morning, after the weekend," Emily told him. She looked over at him in the driver's seat. "Why? Are you worrying?"

"I'd be lying if I said no," Daniel said.

Emily noticed the frown line between his eyebrows then. It seemed to have become deeper in the five days since missing her due date.

"It's normal," Emily reassured him. "I promise you. I was late. I don't remember by how much but these things do run in families."

Daniel's tense expression remained. It seemed as though she'd alleviated none of his concern whatsoever.

"Daniel," she said firmly but without malice. "Why don't you come to the appointment on Monday? Doctor Arkwright will put your mind at ease, I'm sure."

"I'm hoping it won't come to that," he told her. "Hopefully Charlotte will come over the weekend."

"We'll see," Emily replied, feeling quietly confident that she would not.

They drove the short distance to the school. Daniel kept the car at an extremely slow speed, which he put down to the ice, but Emily thought was at least fifty percent because of his anxiety over her continued pregnancy. She couldn't help but wish he'd trust her on this. She knew her body better than he did.

The parking lot at the school was already half full of cars. There were parents filing through the playground and up the steps. Daniel parked up and he and Emily hopped out, then joined the masses.

Yvonne appeared behind them. "I'm so excited!" she cried. "Doctor Seuss is the *best.*" She added in a stage whisper behind her hand. "I also cannot wait to see Laverne Kingsley as Ebenezer Scrooge. She was born for the part, don't you think?"

Emily stifled her chuckle at her friends characteristically cutting wit!

They herd of people ahead of them took another collective step forward, and Emily dutifully inched forward as well. The parents and siblings ahead of them were all wrapped in their winter coats, hats and scarves, but the school's janitor had clearly had the good idea to turn the heating on full blast because they shed them hurriedly the moment they were through the doors. Emily watched in amusement as gloves and hats went flying in a sudden frenzy.

At last they made it inside and discarded their own winter clothes as the blast of heat hit them. The school hall was quite dark when they reached it, with only dim lights to follow to their seats. It was as loud as any town meeting, with all the parents and siblings chatting away happily. In the corner beside the piano, Emily saw a huge Christmas tree covered messily in decorations that the school children had evidently made themselves. A large hand painted sign was stuck to the stage curtain proclaiming; *A Seussified Christmas Carol.*

Emily slipped into her seat beside Daniel. It was much harder to fit in the plastic chairs than it had been at Chantelle's Christmas play last year, Emily realized! It was if Baby Charlotte was stretching to touch the seat in front of her!

Emily took her cell from her purse and nudged Daniel.

"You be on filming duty," she said. "I'm going to try and get my mom and dad on a video call."

Even in the darkness she could tell Daniel's eyebrows had shot a mile up his forehead.

"Is that a good idea?" he said. "Both of them? In the same call?"

"It's fine, Amy showed me how to do it. She has video conference calls all the time for her job and…"

Daniel cut her off. "I don't mean that. I mean, isn't it a recipe for disaster having both your parents in the same space at the same time? Even if that space is virtual."

Maybe once it would have been, for these days Emily felt confident her family had turned a corner. It was quite extraordinary, she thought, to be able to now inhabit that headspace after dozens of years believing her parents would never be in the same place ever again.

"I think it will be fine," she said. "Neither of them know enough about technology to work out what's going on anyway."

She made the call to Patricia first. To her delight, her mom answered as if she'd been ready and waiting for the call.

"Mom," Emily said with a warning tone in her voice. "You'll have to be completely silent throughout, okay. No talking. You're in the audience."

"Yes, yes," Patricia said, impatiently. "I'm not an imbecile. I know how it works"

"Okay. And if the call drops DON'T ring back. Daniel is filming it all and we'll send you that."

"Alright," Patricia replied, absorbing the rules with a slight pout on her lips.

"And one more thing," Emily added. "I'm going to try to get dad to watch too."

Patricia looked startled. "Isn't it the evening in Greece? Won't he be in bed?"

"You're right," Emily confirmed, consulting her clock and adding on the seven hour time difference. "It will be after midnight." She hesitated, thinking of all the calls and messages she'd sent Roy that had thus far gone unanswered. One more certainly wouldn't hurt. Maybe catching him at a strange hour of the day would be just the thing to make him pick up. She had no idea what kind of routine he kept these days anyway. And she knew Roy would love the chance to see Chantelle on stage. "I still think it's worth a shot, though."

Even if the chances of him picking up were slim, she still wanted to try.

Patricia shrugged, nonchalant. "If you think so. I won't have his face in the corner of my screen will I? It will be dreadfully distracting."

"I'll make sure you don't," Emily replied. "Speak later, mom."

She opened up the menu to try and start the conference call, when she heard Patricia speak.

"Emily! Emily!"

She sighed and held the phone up to her face again. "Yes, mom?"

"I've been thinking about Christmas. Chantelle's offer."

"Oh?"

There was a pause. Emily frowned. "And?"

"And what?" Patricia replied bluntly. "I'm just telling you I've been thinking about it."

"Right," Emily said with a sigh. "Okay mom. I'll speak to you later."

She went back to the menu and started tapping buttons. Patricia didn't interrupt this time. She found Roy's details and made the call. There was no answer.

"I told you he'd be in bed," Patricia's disembodied voice said, making Emily startle.

Emily closed down the menu and her mom's face appeared again. "Yes, alright, mom," Emily replied. "You were right. Now shhhhh!"

She turned the screen around to face the stage. Suddenly, the already dim lights faded even more than, until it was pitch black. The audience fell to silence.

"It's not working!" Patricia's voice rang out. "I can't see a thing!"

To the sound of muted chuckles from the seats around her, Emily spun the camera back to face her. She whispered loudly.

"The lights have dimmed because it's starting. And be quiet or I'll end the call!"

She felt Daniel squeeze her arm reassuringly, and she turned the camera back to face the stage. The curtains had opened onto a Christmas scene.

"Oh there she is!" Emily heard Patricia's shrill voice. "There's my darling Chantelle!"

Emily shrunk into her seat and looked over at Daniel. This was going to be a long night!

*

Luckily, there were no more Patricia induced mishaps from that point forward, and Emily quickly relaxed into the play. Chantelle was an absolute star, of course. Her extra singing lessons from Owen had really paid off. Rather than her usual slow, angelic singing, her solo in the play was an upbeat number, and she delivered it with pitch-perfect precision. As the crowd applauded, Emily glanced over at Daniel and grinned as she saw him wipe away a proud tear.

All too soon, the kids were congregated on the stage belting out the final lines to the last song. The play had been utterly delightful, and the moment the song ended, the crowd erupted with applause. Emily found herself suddenly on her feet, cheering and clapping with her hands high above her head, jumping on the spot as though she weren't currently over nine months pregnant!

The curtain fell then and the lights came back on. Emily turned to Daniel and hugged him.

"Wasn't she fantastic?" he gushed.

"She was marvellous," Patricia's voice came from Emily's hand.

Emily startled. She'd forgotten about her! She let go of Daniel and looked at her mom.

"You watched the whole thing," she said, touched. "Chantelle will be so pleased."

"She needed one of her grandparents to watch," Patricia replied a little haughtily.

Emily felt the sting keenly. Why was Roy being so evasive right now? Was he hiding something from her -- a change in his physical appearance or similar -- in order to protect her from his condition? She certainly didn't want him to! She wanted every little ounce of her father fate would allow her.

"I wish he'd answer my calls," Emily said, sadly, quite forgetting that it was Patricia she was seeking solace from.

To her surprise, her mom gave her a caring, sympathetic smile. "I know you do, darling. I'm sure he had a reason for being AWOL. He always had some reason or other in his mind, even if it didn't make that much sense to the people who loved him."

Emily nodded. It wasn't often Patricia could soothe her.

"Mom, the kids are coming out now," Emily said. "I'd better go."

"Send my love to Chantelle."

"I will."

Emily ended the call. Daniel pulled her close to him, offering comfort for the sadness over Roy she was so evidently feeling. Together, they went to collect Chantelle.

They'd just made it out into the gangway, when someone appeared next to Emily.

"Roman!" she exclaimed. "How are you...?"

He grinned widely. There was an enormous bunch of flowers in his arms. "I made it back in time after all," he said. "Wasn't she ace? My Christmas angel!"

"Chantelle will be just thrilled to see you," Emily said. "Come on."

The three of them made it to the collection point. Chantelle had the proudest look on her face ever when she realized her parents were approaching. But then her gaze fell to Roman and a huge grin burst across her face.

"You came!" she cried, throwing her arms around him.

"These are for you," Roman said, handing her the flowers.

Emily laughed as the little girl accepted the bouquet. It was about double her size!

"Thank you so much," Chantelle replied. "They're gorgeous."

"Check the message," Roman added.

Chantelle frowned and pulled out the small card. She cleared her throat and read aloud.

"Dear Chantelle. Would you be kind enough to lend your vocals to my latest Christmas charity single? A recording session will be taking place at my studio tomorrow. RSVP."

Chantelle's eyes were wide with elevation. "What does RSVP mean?"

"It means you have to respond," Roman quipped.

"Oh!" Chantelle laughed. "Then yes! Can I mommy? Daddy?"

Emily and Daniel nodded vigorously. "Absolutely!"

CHAPTER TEN

Terry and Chantelle left for Roman's house bright and early the next morning. Emily waved them off from the door of the inn, wrapped in her dressing gown, holding a steaming mug of cocoa.

"Don't have the baby while I'm gone!" Chantelle called out behind her as she went.

Emily laughed. She was six days overdue and her body was giving her zero indications of wanting Baby Charlotte out. She wasn't worried, knowing that her sister and guardian angel was watching over her. In fact, she was just excited to find out what fate might have instore for her since it had clearly decided to delay her meeting Charlotte.

She went back upstairs to see whether Daniel was still sleeping. The bed was empty and she could hear the sound of the shower going in the en suite bathroom. She sat on her vanity stool, catching her breath from the effort of climbing up the stairs, until he was done.

He emerged from the steaming room with his hair in wet tendrils.

"What's the plan for today?" Emily asked. "Since we're unexpectedly child free."

Daniel rubbed his wet hair with a towel. "I won't be able to convince you to book in with the doctor, will I?"

"Nope," she replied.

"Well then maybe you'd want to come to the Hanukkah service at the synagogue with me?"

"Oh," Emily said, surprised. She'd never been to a service at a synagogue. In fact, she was pretty sure Daniel hadn't either! "Is it allowed? I mean, I'm not Jewish."

Daniel chuckled. "Of course it's allowed. It's not like your ID gets checked on the door! And besides, it's a very liberal synagogue, you know that. Believe it or not, you and I are not the only interfaith couple in the world." He gave her a sarcastic wink.

Emily mulled it over. Daniel's faith seemed to be becoming more important to him as time passed. She wondered if it was a way for him to remain connected to his roots in the absence of his family.

"Hanukkah ends tomorrow," Daniel added. "And I would like to have done at least one thing this year to celebrate it. You don't have to come with me if you're not feeling well enough to but I'd like to go nevertheless."

"I suppose it wouldn't hurt," Emily said finally.

Daniel looked touched that she was making the effort. "Is that a yes?"

"Yes. But on one condition," she added.

Daniel raised a curious eyebrow. "Which is?"

"We walk there."

"Oh," Daniel replied, deflating immediately. "Is that a good idea?" His gaze fell to her ballooning bump. "The sidewalks are still icy. I don't want you to slip."

Emily rubbed her stomach. "We'll be fine. And I should be doing some gentle exercise every day, the doctor said as much." She shrugged. "It's not that far really."

"It's a thirty minute walk!" Daniel told her. He looked concerned. It was becoming his default expression these days. "Which may be perfectly accomplishable for a healthy thirty-something man, but is arguably outside the realms of possibility for a heavily pregnant thirty something woman."

He'd been attempting a light-hearted joke, but Emily wasn't in the mood to receive it.

"I can walk for thirty minutes," she told him, her tone overly sternly. "You need to stop wrapping me up in cotton wool. You treat me like a child sometimes. Just stop worrying."

Daniel frowned, the expression on his face showing Emily that he'd realized she'd not taken his joke well.

"I'll stop worrying when you go into labor," he replied, sounding suddenly serious. "Or at the very least when we visit Doctor Arkwright on Monday and get an induction date."

They fell silent. Emily folded her arms and titled her body away from him. She couldn't help but feel frustrated with Daniel. Though on the one hand she understood why he was nervous, she felt like there was a lot of judgement coming from him. He was taking his worry out on her and it just wasn't fair. She was doing what was best, she was certain of it.

They dressed for the service in silence, then headed downstairs to layer up in their warm winter jackets, hats, scarves and gloves. By the time they were ready to leave, Emily had had just about enough of the silence as she could handle and decided it was time to break the tension.

"It's kind of funny, don't you think?" she said, wiggling her feet into a pair of faux fur lined boots. "That while we're hanging out in a synagogue, our daughter will be recording a song with a famous popstar."

Daniel let out a small smile. But Emily could tell there was no way of alleviating his growing anxiety. And she realized then that until Baby Charlotte arrived, it would only get worse.

*

Emily was right about it getting worse. The next day, Daniel seemed sullen as they ate breakfast around the kitchen table, keeping his nose buried in a copy of the free local newspaper as if it was some kind of protective shield.

"Did you have fun at Roman's yesterday?" Emily asked Chantelle.

The poor kid had been so exhausted when she'd returned home they hadn't really had a chance to speak about it properly.

Chantelle looked up from her clock pieces. She'd long since finished her eggs on toast and, as was now habitual, had turned her attention to her latest construction.

"Oh yes," she said grinning, her eyes wide and expensive. "It was so much fun. I got to meet the producer and the sound mixer. They both had crazy hair styles. Then I went in a booth and wore big headphones to sing. And the microphone had this big black sheildy thing in front of it, which Roman told me is called the pop filter, because when you sing a 'p' sound it makes a loud pop noise on the record. Also they had to press a button to speak to me because the booth was completely soundproof!"

Emily could tell she'd enjoyed herself because she'd barely taken a breath.

"That does sound fun," Emily replied. "What about Terry? Did he enjoy himself as much as you?"

"I think so," Chantelle said. "He's quite shy though. I mean, Roman's producer is really loud and has bright red hair and all these piercings. I think Terry was a bit scared of him." Then she frowned. "Where *is* Terry?"

"He's gone to church," Emily told her. "He left quite early this morning."

Chantelle pondered it. "How come we don't go to church?"

Daniel folded his paper down then, as though he had been secretly listening in all along. "Funny you should mention that. We actually went to the synagogue yesterday, Emily and I, for a Hanukkah service."

"Aww, and I missed it?" Chantelle asked, looked suddenly glum. "I'm sorry, Daddy. I was supposed to celebrate Hanukkah with you. But it's ending today, isn't it?"

Rather than look disappointed to have not shared any Hanukkah celebrations with his daughter, Daniel looked pleased that she'd even remembered. "That's okay, sweety. How about you help me light the last candle on the menorah tonight? We have to wait until after sunset to do it."

Chantelle nodded her excitement. "Okay! And we can play that game again with the spinny dice and candies."

Daniel looked even more touched. "You mean dreidel?"

"Yes! That's the one! And we can make those latkes again like we did last year."

Daniel was grinning from ear to ear now, so clearly touched was he that Chantelle had remembered so much from last year's Hanukkah celebrations.

"Sounds perfect," he said. "Then it will be full steam ahead with the Christmas celebrations."

Chantelle looked a little downcast then. "I don't feel very Christmasy anymore."

"Oh no," Emily said, saddened to hear it. "But why not?"

She shrugged. "I guess now that the play has finished at school, I don't feel like there's anything to look forward to."

"What about Santa?" Emily cried.

"To be honest, I'm much more interested in Charlotte coming than Santa coming," Chantelle replied.

"You and I both," Daniel added without missing a beat.

He shot an accusational glance across the table at Emily. She shifted uncomfortably. Now she felt like she was letting them both down by refusing to fix an induction date. It took all her resolve not to cave.

"Wasn't Charlotte supposed to be here already?" Chantelle continued. There was a hint of a whine in her voice, like she was impatiently waiting for a UPS package to be delivered rather than for her mom to go through the agony of childbirth!

Emily rubbed her stomach. "She's not ready yet," she told them defensively.

"But we're seeing the Doctor tomorrow," Daniel explained to Chantelle. "Then we'll set a date for the induction."

Emily frowned. "I never said I wanted one," she told him. She couldn't help but snap. It was unfair of him to act like they could give Chantelle any answers when Emily herself hadn't made a decision on that yet.

"I thought that was the whole point of seeing Doctor Arkwright," he replied, looking tense. "Why else would be going if not to book in the induction?"

"Because I need to be monitored a little more regularly," she said shrugging, trying to sound nonchalant, knowing full well the news would stress Daniel out even further.

"Are you sick, mommy?" Chantelle asked, looking worried.

"Not at all," Emily assured her. She felt frustrated with Daniel for making his attitude so clear in front of Chantelle. His worry was worrying her in turn, and the last thing Emily needed right now was to absorb vicarious anxiety from the both of them! Especially when she was the one who would soon be doing all the pushing.

"Everything's fine," Daniel said, patting Chantelle's hand on the table. "It's completely normal."

"Remember what Nanna Patty said," Emily added. "I was two weeks late and so was Charlotte!"

"TWO WEEKS," Chantelle moaned. "I can't wait that long!"

Emily rubbed her tummy. "Well you're just going to have to." She looked over at Daniel with an unwavering determination. "Both of you."

*

Monday could not have come soon enough for Daniel, Emily thought when they woke the next day. He seemed to be radiating impatience, hurrying her to dress quicker and eat breakfast quicker and get in the car quicker.

"We'll be early at this rate," Emily told him.

In the back seat of the pickup, Chantelle seemed to be quietly absorbing her parent's stress, watching them curiously as they bickered and snapped at one another. Emily felt very bad about it. She wanted nothing more than to set Chantelle a good example, but Daniel's attitude was certainly making it difficult.

Luckily he didn't drive any quicker than normal. He had been very careful in that respect ever since Emily had reached full term, like he was worried too many bumps and jolts would break her. She wished everyone would stop acting like she was so fragile.

After dropping Chantelle off at school they went onwards to the doctor's office. Their appointment was the first of the day, and when Doctor Arkwright's receptionist saw them arriving she ushered them straight through. Rose Arkwright looked up from her desk as they entered through the door.

"How are you both?" she asked, smiling in her professionally efficient way. "Still very much pregnant, I see, Emily."

Emily laughed. "Yes. And I'm fine. Feeling great, actually. Although I'm not so sure the same can be said for Daniel."

She looked over at him and offered a smile. He didn't look amused, however.

"Oh?" the Doctor asked, turning her attention to Daniel. "What's the worry?"

"I'm concerned about her being overdue," he said tersely. "She's a week past her due date."

"There's nothing to be concerned about," the doctor said, echoing Emily's own sentiment, making her feel validated. "Anywhere between 38 weeks and 42 weeks is considered full term. And only five percent of babies are born on their due date anyway. There's a five week variation in the length of pregnancy. It's entirely normal. And bear in mind that just because we call it a *due* date, we don't necessarily mean it's the *best* date. Emily's body will know when it's ready. It will do what it's supposed to."

Daniel seemed to be put a bit at ease by the doctor's assurances, but Emily thought he looked like his pride had been dented a little. He folded his arms and fell into brooding silence.

Doctor Arkwright turned her attention back to Emily.

"So you're at 41 weeks now," she said, "Which means we ought to do a membrane sweep today to see if we can get things started without chemicals. But I'd recommend we go ahead and book an induction for next Monday morning, just in case, as that will be the 42 week date."

"I'm not sure if I want to be induced," Emily blurted suddenly.

She heard Daniel suck in a sharp breath behind her.

"Okay..." the doctor began, sounding a bit reticent. "Of course, it is your choice but know that my medical advice would be to have an induction on the 42 week mark. Otherwise, we will need to see you every day after 42 weeks, or possibly even admit you into hospital."

"Why would she be admitted?" Daniel asked, sounding panicked.

"There's a slight increased risk of stillbirths with pregnancies that go on beyond 42 weeks," she explained in a calm and diplomatic tone. "Because things can change very quickly with the baby, we may need to monitor her heartbeat and movements and intervene if necessary. A water birth will be off the cards as well."

She looked at Emily again. "Do you understand everything I've told you?"

"I do," Emily said. "And I hope you can see where I'm coming from. I'd really prefer to let nature do its thing. My mom said she was late with both her babies and we were fine."

The doctor replied with a nod. "Like I said, it's your choice. As long as you understand there are risks involved."

Emily couldn't help noticing the way her smile had diminished a little. She dared not look at Daniel's expression. She knew he would not be taking the news very well.

"Let's do our checks shall we?" the doctor said then, picking up a blood pressure cuff.

She slid it up Emily's arm and turned on the machine. Emily felt the familiar sensation of the cuff filling with air, squeezing tightly against her upper arm. Having her blood pressure checked all the time wasn't the most pleasant of experiences, but at least the pain was only temporary. She was getting pretty used to it all now.

A little slip of paper printed out of the attached machine, showing her blood pressure information. The doctor read it and entered the data onto her computer.

"That's all fine," she said. Then she stood. "Can I get you to lay on the bed for me so we can do an ultrasound?"

Emily did as she was asked, pulling up her shirt in preparation for the jelly to be applied. She always felt excited when she knew she was seeing her baby, but she also couldn't help but hope this would be the last time that it was on a screen rather than in real life!

"A bit of jelly coming," Doctor Arkwright said and Emily flinched at the sensation as the cold goo was blobbed onto her belly.

The Doctor began to move the wand through the jelly on Emily's stomach. Emily looked at the screen, seeing the unmistakable shape of her baby. Her spine was clearly visible as was the small black shape that was her beating heart.

"Hmm," Doctor Arkwright said. She was peering at a different screen, one that had information scrolling onto it.

"Hmm what?" Daniel asked, sounding extremely concerned. "Is there something wrong?"

"Baby's heartbeat is a little slow," the doctor said. "One hundred ten beats per minute. It's not *too* low but it is right on the cusp. And it's lower than it has been before."

"What does that mean?" Emily asked.

"It could mean a few things," the doctor explained, removing the wand and wiping it clean. "The first and most obvious one is that you could be approaching labor. A baby's drop in heart rate can be an early indication of that."

"What other things could it mean?" Daniel asked. His voice was very strained, Emily noted.

The Doctor turned the machine off and handed Emily some paper towels to wipe her tummy. She sat up and cleaned herself as Doctor Arkwright took her seat again, swivelling to face them.

"There is a small possibility that it means the baby is getting stressed," she explained. "Again, because your pregnancy is at 41 weeks, it might be that baby is wanting to come out before your body is ready. Either way, I think it would be best if we admitted you to hospital to keep an eye on things."

Emily's heart sunk. Hospital was the last place she wanted to be right now. Especially when she was so certain that everything was fine, and when she was trying so hard to make sure Daniel didn't worry unnecessarily. But she knew Charlotte's health was more important and she would do whatever she had to to keep her child healthy.

"If you think it's for the best," she said.

She looked over at Daniel. He looked terrified.

"It's just a precaution," Doctor Arkwright said, in a clear attempt to reassure him.

"I think Daniel's more worried than I am," Emily said.

"Well someone has to be," Daniel snapped. He paced away, running his hands through his hair.

Doctor Arkwright gave Emily a sympathetic look. She'd had a front row seat to the stresses and strains the pregnancy had put on their marriage. Emily thought she'd probably seen far worse than her and Daniel's bickerings. At least, she hoped she had.

"I'll just make a call to the hospital," the doctor said, swivelling in her chair and picking up the phone.

Whilst she was talking on the phone with her back to them, Emily tried to get Daniel to relax. He was wound as tightly as an elastic band, and she was scared he might snap any second.

"Can you please come and sit down?" she asked. "Pacing won't help anything."

"Nothing will help anything," he said, "Apart from you having our baby. Please Emily. This is turning me into a nervous wreck."

"Daniel," she said, firmly. "You heard what the doctor said. Anything between 38 and 42 weeks is considered full term. I'm not even really overdue. Charlotte isn't in danger. I wouldn't put her in danger. You have to understand that."

"Are you afraid?" he asked. "Of giving birth? Is that why you're delaying it?"

Emily shook her head. She couldn't really explain what was going through her mind, just that there was a reason for everything and if the universe hadn't made her go into labor yet there was surely a good reason for it. She just had to be patient and have faith, and see what fate had in store for her.

"I'm not delaying it," she told him. "It's just not time. I don't know how to explain it to you. I just know, okay?"

Daniel took a deep breath. Emily could tell he was trying to understand, even if it was impossible for him as a man to know what she was experiencing and how she could be so certain of something like that.

"Look, I will have the membrane sweep once we're at hospital, okay?" she said. "Will that make you happy?"

"Happier," he mumbled.

Doctor Arkwright put her phone down then and turned back to face them.

"Okay, so that's all sorted. You're going to the maternity ward in Portland."

"Portland?" Daniel cried. "Why not the local hospital? That's an hour drive away!"

Doctor Arkwright looked surprised. "It's the maternity facility you selected for any prenatal admissions. It's on your forms."

He looked at Emily, frowning. All she could do was shrug.

"I chose it because it offers the best maternity care in Maine," she said. "I suppose I wasn't really think I'd need to be admitted at any point prior to labor. Or at least this close to it."

Daniel let out a long sigh. "Right. Fine," he said, sounding clipped. He held his hand out to the doctor to shake. "Thanks for everything."

She stood and shook his hand. "Please try not to worry. I know as the father-to-be you can feel a bit helpless and out of control. But Emily has got this in hand."

Emily thanked her next, then they left the doctor's office, went outside, and got into Daniel's truck.

"Chantelle's going to be upset," he said as he turned the key in the ignition. "You know how much she worries about you and misses you when you're away."

He was looking over his steering wheel with his jaw tight, rather than at Emily. The truck rumbled beneath them as it idled in the parking lot, spewing out fumes into the cold air.

Emily rubbed her bump protectively. "You sound like you're annoyed with me. Like you think it's my fault I have to go to hospital."

"I'm not," he said. "Don't be ridiculous."

"Ridiculous? You're being so short with me."

"I don't mean to be," he said, sighing. "I just feel so out of control. You're making all the decisions. I feel like a spare part."

"Please just learn to trust me," Emily replied. "It's my body. I know what's best. And pretty soon we'll have our new baby and all of this will be in the past."

But as he reversed the car out of the lot, Daniel remained silent.

CHAPTER ELEVEN

Emily and Daniel drove to the hospital in Portland, which was, indeed, an hour out of Sunset Harbor. Emily desperately wished this wasn't happening and prayed that everything was okay with Baby Charlotte. But no matter how tense she felt, it didn't even bear a patch on Daniel's emotions. He was practically radiating fear. His face was completely drained of color as they drove.

"Honey, you have to calm down," Emily told him. "Nothing bad will happen."

"I can't help it," Daniel replied. "I'm scared. I mean I'm driving you to hospital for Pete's sake. How am I supposed to be relaxed about that?"

Emily touched his arm lightly. "Just try. For my sake. Please."

He nodded and his face relaxed a little. But, Emily noted, his hands were still gripping the steering wheel tightly enough to turn his knuckles white.

Once they made it to the hospital, Daniel parked up and helped Emily into the main foyer. It was a very large, bright building, with all the medical staff wearing friendly pastel colored uniforms rather than clinical whites. There were also lots of plants around and a fish tank filled with tropical fish. Just the atmosphere of the place helped Emily relax immensely.

Daniel went up to the desk.

"This is Emily-Jane Morey. We were sent by Doctor Arkwright."

The nurse at the desk tapped their information into her computer.

"Okay, would you like to come with me," she said, smiling kindly.

They followed her through a corridor to the maternity ward. The sound of newborn's cries echoed through the corridors. Emily felt a surge of excitement, knowing she would soon be in the same position as the new moms on this ward, holding her infant in her arms. Even the shrill cries sounded like music to her ears.

They passed the premature ward, where tiny babies were lying under UV lights in plastic incubators. Emily felt her heart hitch at the sight of them, and was so relieved that Charlotte had chosen to be late rather than early. She wouldn't have been able to cope with such a fragile little thing, and had no idea how much strength it took the parents in there now to see their babies look so small, to feel so helpless. She felt Daniel's hand gripping hers. He was clearly as moved by the sight of the preemies as she was and it felt good to feel like they were united again rather than on opposing sides.

"Right, here's your room," the nurse said, leading them into a bright, clean space.

There was a large bed, a separate en suite bathroom, and all kinds of monitors set up in the room.

"Oh," Emily said, feeling daunted by all the huge pieces of equipment. "This is all for me?"

"Nothing to worry about," the nurse explained. "We're just going to monitor both your heart beats." She pointed at a metal pole on wheels. "This is for an IV line in case you become dehydrated." Then she pointed to a machine with a long tube coming from it, with a mouthpiece attached to the end. "And this is the gas and air, just in case we're meeting your little one today." She winked. "Now, I'll leave you to get undressed. Your gown is on the bed."

She left the room and Emily began to change. It made her feel much more vulnerable to be in the thin hospital gown rather than her own clothes, much more like a patient than a person. And she couldn't stop looking at all the machines. They were so large, so clinical looking. Their presence made her anxious. Even though she knew in her gut that nothing was wrong with Charlotte, seeing all that complicated machinery made her worry that her instincts might be wrong.

After a short while, there was a knock on the door and the nurse came back in.

"I'm just going to put this tag on your wrist," she said to Emily, affixing a clear plastic bracelet around her arm, that had her name written upon it.

Now Emily really began to feel bad.

"Am I being admitted overnight?" she asked. The only time she'd ever had a bracelet before was when she'd had to stay overnight.

"Didn't Doctor Arkwright explain?" the nurse asked. "Whenever we have a woman admitted with a low fetal heart rate we monitor them for twenty four hours minimum. It's the only way we can see whether the rate is low because of distress or just low naturally. And it's the best way we can assess the movement of your baby."

"But she's moving fine," Emily said, cradling her stomach defensively. "Just as much as she always does."

"It's not always easy for moms to detect a change in movement," the nurse explained. "That's what the machines can do for us. I'm sorry, I appreciate it's a bit of a frustration to be in this position. But I can arrange for a membrane sweep once I've taken your bloods, and that will certainly help speed things along. Obviously if she's born we won't need to keep you in to monitor her!"

Emily nodded. She didn't look at Daniel though, assuming his expression would be smug.

She sat on the large hospital bed, which was covered with crisp white sheets that smelled of cleaning fluids, and sat patiently as the nurse took her blood. It was painful but Emily was used to it now. Nine months of being pricked and prodded had made her pretty hardy. Besides, her mind was elsewhere, mulling over the way the nurse had implied that mom's couldn't always detect changes to their baby's movements. She knew Baby Charlotte better than she knew herself. Every twitch and kick had registered with her, from the routine way she woke at dusk, to the way she slept whenever Emily showered, to the way it always felt like she was practising boxing after breakfast. Emily knew all that stuff intimately, she didn't need a machine to tell her it!

Once the blood test was over, the nurse left with the vials, promising to return shortly.

As soon as she was gone, Emily turned to Daniel.

"This is terrible timing," she said. "It's the last few days of school for Chantelle. I'm supposed to be sending in cookies for their charity bake sale."

"I can make cookies," Daniel told her. Then, he changed his mind. "I mean I can buy them from the store. Is that allowed?"

Emily sighed. "Yes. But it's not the same, is it? She'll be so disappointed."

"Don't worry about Chantelle," Daniel told her. "Focus on yourself and the baby. Take care of that."

Emily thought he was being remarkably diplomatic, considering she could potentially resolve this situation by agreeing to being induced. But it didn't feel right to rush it. Despite the setback, she still felt certain that she wanted to wait.

"If you're staying overnight, I should go home and pick some stuff up for you. Is there anything you need in particular?" Daniel asked Emily.

"Books," she said. "Really trashy ones. Oh, and maybe Bryony? We were supposed to be having a meeting later today."

"Well that's definitely not happening," Daniel said, rolling his eyes. "I'm only bringing you non-work related things."

"But we're supposed to be working out the winter marketing deals," she explained. "You know, because the inn hasn't got any bookings over winter at all!"

"It will just have to wait," Daniel told her. "Until you're well enough."

Emily knew he was right, but she hated the idea of lying around like some kind of damsel in distress. It was infuriating. And she definitely didn't want Daniel thinking he'd been right to worry!

"I'd better go," Daniel said then. "The weather report is saying more snow. I don't want to get caught in a ton of traffic and miss picking Chantelle up from school." He leaned down and kissed her. "Take care, won't you, while I'm gone? I'll be back with Chantelle asap."

Emily nodded, sadly, wishing he didn't have to leave her. But knowing he'd be back shortly with Chantelle stopped her from becoming too unhappy.

Daniel left, waving goodbye, and a little while later, the nurse came back.

"Right, let's get all these machines hooked up," she said.

She attached Emily to all the large machines, and Emily listened to the sound of Charlotte's heart beat in the background. Her own heart beat was displayed on a large screen beside her.

"Is everything okay?" she asked.

"Yes," the nurse said. "She's at one hundred and sixteen beats, so she hasn't dropped. That's a good sign."

Emily let out a sigh of relief. "What next?"

"Next," the nurse said, turning her attention from the chart she was writing on to Emily's eyes, "Is to arrange for your membrane sweep. Are you okay for me to organize that now? Have an OB GYN sent in?"

Emily hesitated. "Actually, my husband has just left," she said. "Can we wait until he's back? I'd hate to go into labour with him a whole hour's drive away."

The nurse nodded. "Of course. We can wait until he's back. You rest up. I'll be back in a few hours to check everything again. If you need anything in the meantime, press this bell."

Emily nodded her understanding and the nurse left her. She decided the best way to pass the next few hours until Daniel and Chantelle arrived was to nap. At 41 weeks pregnant, the urge to fall asleep at random points during the day was quite hard to fight, and now she'd more or less been given a free pass to not fight at all.

Napping in a big, clean bed in a quiet place was a temptation she could not resist!

She rested a hand across her stomach and said a silent prayer for Baby Charlotte. Then she felt a kick against her hand as if in response, and smiled, knowing that everything would be okay.

*

When she woke, it was dark. The nurse was hovering by her bedside, checking the monitors beside her.

"What time is it?" Emily murmured, trying to sit up.

"I'm sorry, did I wake you?" the nurse replied. She checked her watch. "It's seven p.m."

"Oh," Emily gasped, quickly sitting all the way up. "I was expecting my husband and daughter to come straight here after school. They should be here by now."

"I expect the snow's held them up," the nurse replied.

"Snow?" Emily asked.

"It's been snowing the whole while you've been asleep," the nurse said, smiling.

She drew the blinds up for Emily then. Emily gasped as she set eyes upon the thick white snow piled up outside her window. A matter of hours earlier there had been no snow at all, and the weather forecast had only indicated that some might come, not that thick layers would fall!

"They put out a notice to not drive," the nurse added.

"For how long?" Emily gasped, thinking of Daniel and Chantelle. The thought of spending the whole evening and night at hospital alone was daunting.

"I think it might be all night now," the nurse said. "The temperature just keeps dropping. But try not to worry about that."

"I can't help it," Emily said, seeing her heart rate on the monitor increasing in time to her panic. "What about the sweep? I can't have it now if they won't be able to come!"

Giving birth alone with them stuck over an hour away from her was a terrifying prospect!

"We don't have to do it," the nurse said, giving her a sympathetic look. "All your tests are coming back fine. Let's just relax. I'll bring you some food and some books. Enjoy the quiet. No one will make you do anything you don't want to do."

Her words bought some comfort to Emily. But this snow had come out of nowhere, taken her by surprise. And she'd not yet seen a forecast for the following day.

101

"Do you know if it will be clear by tomorrow?" she asked. "What's the forecast?"

The nurse looked a bit guilty then. "I'm afraid there's more snow forecast."

Emily felt her worry immediately intensify. "Am I going to be stranded here?"

What if she was left alone all that time? What if she went into spontaneous labor while her family were stuck at home with the roads closed by snow?

"We'll take good care of you," the nurse explained. "Don't worry."

But this time her assurances provided little comfort to Emily. She felt suddenly cut off, isolated. She'd never felt so alone.

"I need to call my family," Emily said.

"Of course," the nurse told her. "You won't be able to use your cell phone but there's a pay phone for patients just down the corridor. Come on, I'll unhook you from the machines and show you the way."

Emily looked over at Baby Charlotte's heart rate monitor. "Is that allowed?"

"If you keep the call short, it won't be a problem at all," the nurse told her kindly.

She helped disentangle Emily from the machines, then offered her arm for Emily to get out of bed. They left Emily's room and walked along the brightly lit corridor. Every room they passed seemed to have loads of people inside them, the mothers and their newborns surrounded by family and friends, bright balloons and gifts. Only she was alone, Emily realized, with her family trapped on the other side of the snow storm.

"Here you go," the nurse said, showing Emily to a phone attached to the wall, with a chair beside it and a plastic hood above it.

It reminded Emily of prison.

"Thank you," she said to the nurse.

She picked up the phone, slotted some coins into it, then dialled the inn. She was relieved that it was Daniel who answered the call.

"Oh sweetheart," he said, sounding utterly relieved. "I was trying to get in touch with you but your cell phone kept going to voicemail. When I called the hospital direct they said you were sleeping."

"I was," Emily said, feeling her voice warble suddenly in her chest. "Are you stuck at home because of the snow?"

"Well, they've issued a warning not to drive," Daniel told her. "But we'll come if you need us to. I won't miss the birth of my daughter because of snow! What happened with the sweep?"

"I didn't have it," Emily told him. "I couldn't bear the thought of you not being here for the birth."

"Well, they said to travel only if it was essential. I think you going into labor counts, don't you? I'll just drive very, very carefully."

"I would prefer you not to put yourself and Chantelle in any danger," Emily said, shaking her head, a desperate feeling in her chest. She felt so torn, wanting her family with her but hating the idea of them being in any danger. "Perhaps if I was in the local hospital it would be a different story. But since you'd be driving for so long, I'd be worrying the entire time." She sighed with sadness. "It's better to stay where you are."

Daniel let out a relieved exhalation. "Okay, I'm going to confess that I'm actually glad you didn't go ahead with the sweep. I really would not have wanted to have to drive out in this weather!"

Emily rolled her eyes. After all his cajoling for her to be induced, he was finally on her side. It had just taken a snowstorm to do it!

"Then fingers crossed I don't go into spontaneous labor," she said, a little wrly.

"Yes," he replied. "For one night only, I will hope for that too."

"Is Chantelle okay?" Emily asked then, wanting to change the subject.

"Other than missing you, she's fine," Daniel said. "Do you want to speak to her?"

Emily checked the clock. She wasn't certain how long she could safely be detached from Charlotte's heart rate monitor, but she desperately wanted to hear Chantelle's voice.

"Yes, quickly," she said. "I need to get back to my machines asap."

"Okay, darling," Daniel said, tenderly. "I love you. I'll be with you the second I can."

Emily's heart lurched. She fought back tears. "I love you too."

There was a moment of silence then, before a rustling sound as Chantelle came on the line.

"Mommy, are you okay?" her sweet little angel voice sang out.

"I'm okay," Emily replied, feeling tears forming in her eyes at the sound of her daughter. "I miss you, that's all."

"I miss you too. When are you coming home?"

"Not tonight," Emily explained. "There's too much snow on the road."

"Daddy and I can shovel a path," Chantelle said innocently.

Emily swallowed her pain.

"That's very kind of you," she managed to say, "But it might take you a very long time. You'll get cold hands."

"We'll wear gloves."

Emily fought to keep her voice even. "Best not to worry. The snow will melt soon enough."

"By tomorrow?"

"Let's hope so," Emily said.

She could only pray that it would.

Emily was about to say farewell to Chantelle, when the child spoke again.

"Are you sure you're okay, mommy?" she asked in a quiet, timid voice. "It's just that I overheard daddy on the telephone to Papa Roy's friend Vladi. And I know you promised only to call him in an emergency. So… is this an emergency?"

Emily's heart clenched even more. "It's not an emergency," she said. "Daddy probably thought I was going to have Baby Charlotte today and wanted Vladi to tell Papa Roy. That's all."

"Promise?"

"I promise."

There was a long pause. Then finally, Chantelle spoke for the last time.

"Okay. I love you mommy. Try not to get too lonely tonight."

"I won't," Emily told her.

But the moment the call ended, she put her head in her hands and wept.

CHAPTER TWELVE

Tuesday passed Emily by in a blur. She felt as if she spent the entire day staring out the window at the unrelenting snow, trying not to cry, wishing it would just stop already. She felt so lost and lonely, and missed her family desperately.

When the nurse came to take some blood, Emily looked up at her with hopeful eyes.

"When will I be discharged?" she asked. "It's my daughter's last day of school tomorrow before the vacation and I really want to be there for her."

The nurse shook her head, sympathetic to her plight, but unmoving. "I'm sorry. It just wouldn't be safe. Even if the snow was cleared we'd want to keep you in for at least another twenty four hours."

Emily's heart sank. This was just awful. Hospitals weren't the nicest places on earth to begin with, and having no family or friends around made it even more bleak. Not to mention the fact that Christmas was fast approaching.

"I've not finished my gift shopping," Emily said, sadly.

The nurse squeezed her shoulder kindly. "I don't think your family is going to mind a few less gifts when its your baby's health that's at stake. Try to relax."

Emily nodded. She knew that relaxing right now was the most important thing she could do, especially if she wanted to avoid having her labor chemically induced. But that was easier said than done.

"I don't know how," Emily said. "I feel like I'm about to cry any second. What if I'm stuck in here over Christmas?"

The nurse gave her a sad, sympathetic look. But she didn't refute it, and Emily faced the very real possibility that she'd be spending Christmas this year alone in a hospital bed. Her tears began to fall.

*

Emily was awake and fretting as the clock ticked past midnight. It was officially Christmas Eve. She grit her teeth, feeling determined. Today she would go home, no matter what. Even if they advised her not to, she was going to discharge herself. She wanted to spend Christmas at home with her family, even if that ran the risk of her giving birth on the dining room floor!

The nurse wasn't scheduled to come and see her until 6 a.m. so there was nothing to do but try and get some rest. But Emily's mind was racing. Was she being a fool, taking a gamble with her health? With her baby's health? Or was she just listening to her own body and her own needs? Being in hospital wasn't doing her any favors. She felt tense here, and very lonely, and knew that the stress would be more harmful for the baby than her being happy and relaxed at home would. Women had carried babies to term for centuries without machines and monitors. If they could do it, she could too.

Somehow she slept, though as she dreamed, her mind was chaotic and filled with anxiety.

When she woke, daylight was streaming in through the curtains.

"Crap!" Emily said, realizing she'd slept straight through the nurse's morning check. The clock read nine a.m.

Just then, the door opened. Emily was prepared with her speech, ready to explain why she needed to be discharged. But it wasn't the nurse who came in. It was Daniel and Chantelle.

"Oh!" Emily exclaimed, breaking down immediately into tears as the two rushed at her. "You're here."

She shuddered with relief. Chantelle held her tightly.

"Don't cry, mommy!" the girl said in a soothing voice.

"I'm so sorry," Emily said, wiping her tears away. "I wasn't expecting to see you. It's just a shock."

Chantelle let go and grinned at her. "Happy Christmas Eve."

Emily wiped her hair from her eyes. "Happy Christmas Eve. Tell me, how was your last day at school?"

"It was fun!" Chantelle said. "We did our talent show. Laverne did a really cool ballet dance. I sang. But Bailey won. She did a comedy routine."

"That sounds like fun," Emily said. She smiled at Daniel. "And the bake sale?"

Daniel nodded. "Chantelle and I made cookies, didn't we sweety?"

"Yes," she said, smiling proudly. "I showed Daddy what to do."

Daniel nodded in affirmation.

Emily felt a surge of gratitude. Her family were here, at last, and everything had been fine in her absence. The inn hadn't fallen down, no one had crashed in the snow. Her worries were finally over.

"I thought you might have had the baby by now," Chantelle commented sadly, seeing Emily's round stomach was still very much there.

"I'm glad I didn't," Emily told them. "Imagine if I'd given birth all alone? It would have been the worst."

Daniel reached out for her hand then. "Did you have the sweep?"

She shook her head. "I didn't want to. Not if you weren't going to be here."

"How about we organize for it to be done now?" he said.

She chewed her lip. "I really just want to go home. I'm sorry. It's Christmas Eve. I don't want to choose to spend it in hospital. I'd prefer to be home if nature allowed." She squeezed Daniel's hand, hoping he could understand where she was coming from. "Once Christmas is over, I promise I'll book in the induction if she's still not come. Okay?"

Daniel exhaled loudly. "This isn't a fight I'm going to win," he said, finally. "You do what's best for you."

"Does that mean mommy's coming home?" Chantelle asked, looking hopeful.

"Yes, I suppose it does," Daniel relented.

Chantelle punched the air with joy. Just then the nurse came in.

"Hello everyone," she smiled, looking around the room. "I see your family made it in the end."

Emily nodded. She was about to launch into her prepared speech about needing to be released, when the nurse beat her to it.

"Now the doctors have agreed to discharge you," she began.

Emily gasped. "They have?"

The nurse nodded. "Yes. All your tests have come back fine. Baby is happy and healthy, no signs of distress. They think it would be better for you to spend Christmas at home rather than in hospital. So you get to go home."

She grinned, evidently aware of how good that news was for Emily. Emily was, indeed, thrilled by the news.

"Thank you," she squealed, sounding breathless with delight.

"Now there is one condition," the nurse added. "Monday, December 28 is when you reach 42 weeks. After that you'll need daily monitoring. So nine a.m. every morning with Doctor Arkwright."

"That's fine by me," Emily said.

She couldn't leave the hospital soon enough. Chantelle helped pack up her things for her, speeding round the room picking up discarded socks and random items that had fallen from her purse, slinging them hastily inside.

"Who has scissors?" Emily said, holding up her plastic name tag. "I want to get this thing off!"

The nurse chuckled and came over with a small pair of scissors. She clipped the tag and discarded in the trash can.

"Thank you!" Emily cried. "For everything!"

Then they were off, heading out into the freezing December air.

Emily almost squealed with delight when she saw Daniel's beat up pick up truck in the parking lot. She was finally going home!

CHAPTER THIRTEEN

It was only when Daniel turned the truck onto the driveway leading up the inn that Emily realized the extent of chaos the snowfall had caused. The roofs of several of the old outhouses had collapsed under the weight of snow. Both the greenhouses had also been crushed.

"Your plants," Emily gasped, looking from Chantelle to Daniel. "All that work you put in with Papa Roy."

"I know," Chantelle said sadly. "And the worse thing is he won't be here to help me fix it all."

Daniel spoke up then. "We're going to make it a spring project, aren't we Chantelle? To have everything fixed up for then. We'll get stronger glass next time around, just in case. George will know the best type to use."

Chantelle nodded, and gazed out the window at the wrecked greenhouses as they parked up. Emily's wish for her father grew even stronger then. She couldn't help but share in the child's sadness that he'd not been in touch or let them know about his plans. Despite Vladi's reassurances, she couldn't help but worry.

"Why don't I help out, Chantelle?" she said. "I've been stuck inside for so long, I'd quite like to have something to do. Something to get my hands dirty with." Noticing Daniel's expression, she added, "I won't do any heavy lifting, don't worry! Just some tidying. Sweeping and raking leaves, that sort of thing. I mean, we can't leave them like that. It's a health and safety hazard and it looks awful."

They all got out of the car and went into the inn. Emily felt so relieved to be home, even if there was some destruction to deal with. Even the smell of the place felt comforting and familiar to her.

"Let's see if Terry can help us with the greenhouse work," Daniel said.

"What about Stu and the others?" Emily asked.

"They've gone home for Christmas," Daniel told her.

"Oh. Of course," Emily replied. She felt sad to have not had a chance to say goodbye and wish them each an enjoyable vacation. She'd gotten so used to having them around the inn they almost felt like family now.

Daniel went off upstairs to fetch Terry. They both came down a little while later.

"Emily, I'm so happy to see you," Terry said, kindly, offering her a gentle hug. "It's just not been the same around here without you."

"Thanks," she said, smiling as she echoed his sentiments. "I've missed this place so much. And you."

They headed outside then and began first by clearing the debris from the greenhouse in Trevor's grounds. Daniel and Terry took on most of the heavy lifting work, with Chantelle mainly acting like the manager. Emily was on hand with a broom to sweep away broken shards of glass and salvage as many plants as she could. With everyone working together, the work was much less laborious. Emily was even enjoying herself. It was much better than being cooped up in a hospital bed after all!

Once the fallen debris was removed, they got a much better sense of the destruction. Many of the plants had been completely flattened, the pots they'd been growing in crushed. The bench was fine, but the stone bird bath had snapped off at its base. Luckily, the fruit trees they'd planted in Trevor's memory had survived.

"Look at this," Chantelle said, suddenly.

Everyone went over to see what she was indicting. Beneath her right foot, there was a wooden trap door.

"Was that always there?" Chantelle asked, blinking up at her parents and Terry.

Emily frowned. "It must have been. But it was covered by something so we didn't notice. Do you think Trevor knew about it?"

She couldn't imagine the meticulously organized man to have missed something like a secret trap door in his greenhouse. Would there be a basement beneath? It was most unusual!

"Trevor must have known," Chantelle said. "He knew about everything."

"I wonder what's down there?" Terry said.

"There's only one way to find out," Daniel replied.

He crouched down and tugged on the large round, rusty handle of the trapdoor. It resisted at first, and he tugged again, straining. This time, it creaked upwards. A cloud of dust and mildewed air gushed out.

"I wonder how long it's been since it was opened!" Emily exclaimed. She was a mixture of thrilled and terrified.

"What's down there, daddy?" Chantelle asked, bouncing on her tiptoes with excitement.

Daniel frowned. "I can see wooden steps leading down. It looks like it was a pantry once. Somewhere to store vegetables over winter."

"How exciting!" Chantelle squealed, clapping her hands. "Can we go down and look?"

"Yes, but we'll need flashlights," Daniel said. "There don't appear to be any windows and it's very dark."

Terry went back to the house with Daniel to collect flashlights, and once every one had one, they began to follow the steps down into the darkness. Thought they creaked beneath each footstep they seemed sturdy.

"It smells funny down here," Chantelle said. "Like old stew."

"That will probably be because of all the potatoes that got stored in here once," Daniel said, and he flashed his light onto a hessian sack with the word POTATOES written upon it in thick, black writing. "Look at that! It's like a relic from a museum."

Just then, they heard Chantelle gasp from behind them. Emily's first thought was a spider's web and she tensed. But then she remembered Chantelle wasn't scared of spiders and so something else had made the child gasp.

She braced herself before turning. But when she looked, she saw that Chantelle's flashlight was on a wooden shelving unit that took up the entirety of one wall. And on every single inch of every single shelf was a piece of silver crockery. Dulled from the dust, but clearly silver.

"What on earth…?" Emily said beneath her breath.

They all hurried forward. Emily's hand fell first to a silver teapot, Daniel's to a large serving platter with designs carved into it. Chantelle found a gravy boat whilst Terry held up a collection of serving spoons. Then Daniel reached up to the highest shelf and pulled down two beautiful butter dishes shaped like shells. From the lowest shelves, Chantelle held up fruit basket, then a soup dish, and finally a collection of drinking goblets. They didn't need an antiquarian to tell them that they were holding precious antiques made of solid silver.

Emily's mouth fell open as she turned the teapot over in her hands. She'd seen such teapots before and knew immediately it was an original, from the Victorian era. It, alone, would be worth thousands. But the collection included even more rare items, like the soup dish which would fetch over ten thousands dollars on its own.

"There's so much of it," she exclaimed. "And to think Trevor kept it a secret!"

Chantelle was so excited. "There's enough here to help Terry rebuild his house and farm."

Terry looked stunned. "Oh, gosh. I couldn't take any. It's not mine. It's your silver on your property."

"But you helped us find it," Chantelle said.

Emily spoke next. "Chantelle's right. It would only be fair to share this. Why don't I call Rico and see if he'd be able to value it all?"

They went back into the inn, and whilst Daniel made coffee, Emily called Rico, the ancient man who owned the local antiques store. Her hands were shaking as she did so.

"It's definitely real silver," she told him. "In need of a polish but all in great condition otherwise. I think it's a complete set."

"Is there a name on any of the pieces?" Rico asked.

"There are initials on the bottom of each piece," Emily told him. "WG. Does that mean anything to you?"

Rico gasped. "I wonder if it's the mark of William Gamble. He was one of the group of infamous Soho silversmiths."

"I've heard that name before," Emily said, nodding with excitement. Though her interest in antiques was nowhere near as extensive as Roy's or Rico's, she knew enough to recognize some of the more prominent people.

"I'm sure you would have," Rico agreed. "He was an English silversmith working in the seventeen hundreds. Popular amongst the royals. Though his aren't especially rare, they sell for thousands of dollars. And you're quite *sure* it's WG? Not EG? He had family members in the trade as well you see, though his are considered more collector's items."

"I'm positive!" Emily exclaimed. "It's WG."

It was a Christmas miracle. To think all this time they'd been sitting on hundreds of thousands of dollars worth of antique silver. There would be enough, once shared between them all, for Terry's house to be rebuilt and his business to start again.

"Do you know anyone who'd want to buy it?" Emily asked Rico.

"You mean other than every antique dealer in the world?" Rico chuckled in reply. "I'll pass some details on to you of some of the best auction houses in Maine. There's a wonderful one specializing in silver. Sutcliff's I think it's called. I'll call them first. Oh Elody, this is wonderfully exciting!"

Emily didn't bother correcting his mistake over her name. Rico had never been able to remember her name, even if he could remember every single last detail about antiques! Instead, she wished Rico a Happy Christmas and ended the call, thrilled by the news.

As she went off in search of her family to tell them the good news, she realized she was more happy for Terry than herself. He'd gone through so much misfortune, it was about time he had something good to look forward to.

*

Emily settled down on the couch that evening, tucking her feet up beneath her. A steaming mug of Daniel's speciality hot chocolate sat on the coffee table before her, and the dogs snoozed beside the lit fireplace. She felt more relaxed and at peace than she had in days.

Daniel and Chantelle crept into the room then, carrying a tray. Emily sat up straight, craning to see what was upon it.

"Cookies," Chantelle said. "The ones we made while you were in hospital."

"Oh look, they're adorable!" Emily cried, looking at the roughly reindeer-shaped cookies. She took one off the tray and bit into it. It made a loud cracking noise.

Chantelle and Daniel looked at her expectantly, clearly waiting for her evaluation. Emily chewed hard, her teeth crunching against the brittle cookie, and made the silent assessment that wasn't anywhere near enough sugar in it.

"It's delicious," she said allowed, swallowing cookie chards with great effort.

She noticed then that there was something else on the tray. A card. She picked it up. It was hand drawn by Chantelle.

"Is that me?" Emily asked, as she studied the extremely pregnant looking stick figure depicted on the front, who was covered in sequins and glitter.

"Yup," Chantelle said. "And that's Charlotte."

She pointed at the huge belly. Emily noticed that she's stuck two googly eyes onto it and chuckled.

"It's beautiful, sweety. Thank you. I'm so happy to be home. Back with you all."

"I just wish Papa Roy was here," Chantelle said, glumly. "And Nana Patty."

"I know, hun," Emily said, smoothing her fingers through the girl's hair. "But if they want to spend Christmas alone, we have to respect that."

113

Chantelle looked up at her then. "I called him again," she blurted, like it was a secret she'd been keeping. "After daddy did. He didn't answer but I left a voicemail about how you were in hospital and needed him."

"You did?" Emily asked, shocked. Part of her felt proud of Chantelle for being so confident and bold. But she also worried to hear what she'd done. She didn't want her father to be concerned about her. In his fragile state it wasn't like there was anything he could do about it.

Just then, there was a ring at the doorbell. Chantelle's eyebrows shot up.

"It won't be him," Emily told her, not wanting her hopes to be raised then dashed.

"But who else would it be?" Chantelle said, suddenly spirited as she headed for the door. "We're not expecting visitors are we? I mean, it's Christmas Eve, everyone will be at home!"

Daniel helped Emily up from the couch and they followed Chantelle out the room and along the corridor. She was already waiting by the door for them, and the bell rang again, causing her to flap her arms like an impatient chicken.

When they reached the door, Daniel opened it.

Emily's gaze fell to the figure standing before her. She blinked once, then twice, not believing it. She even rubbed her eyes, expecting the mirage before her to disappear. But the person on her doorstep was still there when she opened them again. It was her father. It was Roy.

"Dad!" Emily screamed. She threw herself into his open arms.

Chantelle squealed loudly, jumping up and down like Papa Roy was Santa Claus himself.

"What are you doing here?" Emily exclaimed, clutching onto her father.

"Vladi told me Daniel had called," Roy replied. "Then I got Chantelle's message. When I heard you were in hospital I realized I had to be here. It wasn't fair to expect you to come and visit me once Charlotte arrived. I needed to be here for you."

"Oh dad," Emily cried, and her tears began to fall, staining the front of his shirt.

Finally, he released her, and Chantelle immediately occupied the vacant space, hugging him tightly.

"I'm so happy you're here," she gushed. "This is going to be the best Christmas ever."

Daniel reached over and gripped Roy's shoulder in one of his hands, squeezing to express his love and gratitude.

At last Emily understood why Charlotte hadn't been in a hurry to be born. She'd wanted her Papa Roy here to meet her. Fate always had a way of making things work out, she realized.

"Come in, out of the cold, the fire's on!" Emily said, ushering her father inside, staring at him like he was worth more than all the silver in Trevor's pantry ten times over.

"I think this calls for some hot cocoa," Daniel said.

"And roasted chestnuts," Emily added.

"And songs around the piano," Chantelle said.

Everyone laughed, gazing adoringly at Papa Roy as they led him into the warm, firelit living room. Roy was here. It really was a Christmas miracle.

CHAPTER FOURTEEN

Once the initial excitement of Roy's appearance died down, Emily could see how much more frail he was. It must have been a shock to his body to fly all the way here. She understood now why he'd been so resistant to her messages. He must have felt terrible about letting them all down, but clearly he hadn't had much choice. He was too sick to travel. The fact he'd even made it here seemed like a miracle, indeed, and Emily felt so grateful for her emergency hospital visit; however unpleasant the experience had been, it had been the catalyst that had finally brought her father to her side.

Chantelle had fallen asleep on the couch, so Daniel scooped her up and left with her in his arms, to put her in bed, leaving just Emily and her father alone.

From the couch beside her, Roy reached across and patted her hand. "How overdue are you now Emily-Jane?"

"My due date was the 13th and I'm eleven days past that now. But I'm not 42 weeks yet so I'm not really considered overdue. I still fall within the bracket of full term."

"What happens on Sunday then? It will be the last day of being full term, won't it? What if she still hasn't arrived by then?"

"Then I see my doctor each morning for check ups until she comes."

"Gosh," Roy said. "You must be extremely uncomfortable."

"Honestly, it's not as bad as it has been," Emily told him. "When I was throwing up all the time in the first trimester it was much worse. Now it's just a case of moving around being somewhat difficult, and heavy, but I'm not in pain or anything. I'm sure that will all change on Sunday." She smiled wanly. Then she turned her concern back on him. "But how are you, dad? Really? I know you've been avoiding speaking to me."

Roy looked ashamed. "I'm sorry. I didn't want to worry you at these late stages."

Emily sighed. "Do you understand that I worry more when I don't hear from you? We all do. But I'm glad you're okay. And here."

Roy nodded. "It's been a very trying time for me. I made a decision, a medical one, and needed some time to process it all."

Emily recalled what Vladi had told her on the phone, that Roy was in the process of dealing with something and needed time alone to process it. She grew concerned.

"What decision? What are you talking about?"

Roy hesitated for a moment, as if deliberating over whether he should divulge it to her. Then finally, having grappled with his decision, he spoke. "I've signed an AND. Do you know what that means?"

Emily shook her head.

Roy continued, explaining to her. "It stands for Allow Natural Death. It's a prefered term by patients, a more positive term to replace the old medical version, DNR."

Emily's heart clenched. She'd seen another medical television programs to know what DNR meant. It was an abbreviation for Do Not Resuscitate. Her father had essentially made a declaration to forgo an kind of rescuitation intervention. In the event of a medical emergency, first responders or hospital staff dealing with him would not be allowed to perform CPR, heart defibulation, or adrenaline shots. Essentially, he'd made it so that no one could intervene to save his life should his heart give out at any point.

"Why?" she asked, feeling tears welling in her eyes. The news had stung her. It felt like a betrayal, like a refusal to fight. "Why would you want to just give up like that?"

"Look at me," Roy said, sadly, indicating to his bony body. "It wouldn't be like how it is on television. It's not like I'd bounce back to a healthy life. My body wouldn't be able to heal itself. Any extra time it gave me would only be temporary. It would only prolong my pain."

"And that's not worth it?" Emily asked, sounding hurt. "It's not worth it for one more day with us? With me?"

She began to weep loudly. Roy reached for her, drawing her into his arms like a little girl. He held her as she sobbed, and spoke into the crown of her head.

"If it's my time to go, it's my time to go. I would prefer to fall asleep one night and not wake up, then go through even more painful procedures in order to pass away a little later without dignity. That is why we prefer the term AND. Allow natural death. It's about acceptance, about respecting the cycle of life and death. We must all go one day, and I am choosing to give that choice to fate, for it to be the way nature intends rather than prolonging it just because we have the medical advancements to do so. "

With her ear pressed against his heart, Emily listened to his words rumbling through his chest, trying to understand where he was coming from. She couldn't begin to imagine how difficult his day to day life must be if an earlier death was preferable to a prolonged life.

Roy continued speaking to her softly, like she was a little child. "I'm sorry, sweetheart. I didn't want to cause you any more pain. That's why I didn't tell you. But do you understand why I want it that way? Why I want to put my faith into the natural order of things?"

There was nothing to be done about it, Emily realized. Roy had made his choice. If his heart failed before the cancer claimed him, it would all be over. He'd given himself the option of a sudden, abrupt death rather than a slow, painful wasting away. Who was Emily to challenge that decision? He knew his body and his needs better than she. It was what she'd been trying to tell Daniel all along with her pregnancy. It wouldn't be fair not to respect Roy's wishes when she demanded everyone respect hers. He knew what was best for him. He wanted to put his faith in fate, not medicine. Hadn't she been demanding the same thing by refusing to be induced?

"I understand," she whimpered. "It's just so unfair."

"I know."

Her tears stopped flowing then. She sat up and blinked the wet from her lashes.

"We'd better have the best Christmas ever," she told him.

Roy smiled and ran his hand along her cheek tenderly. "I'm absolutely certain we will."

*

Chantelle woke them early the next morning, running through the house screaming, "IT'S CHRISTMAS!"

She was so loud, Emily could hear the dogs barking in the laundry room, woken far earlier than they were used to.

Emily rolled out of bed and was on her feet by the time her bedroom door burst open.

There stood Chantelle, dressed in her pajamas, her hair an absolute state.

"Which room is Papa Roy in?" she demanded.

"Good morning to you, too," Emily said, laughing. "He's in the bridal suite."

She'd insisted on her father having the biggest, grandest, most comfortable room in the whole inn. Unlike Terry, he'd actually accepted, putting his comfort over the virtue of modesty.

Without saying another word, Chantelle ran out of the room. Emily padded after her and called down the corridor, "Don't forget to wake Terry as well!"

She realized Terry and her father had not had a chance to meet yet. Terry had been staying out of their way on Christmas Eve. Despite everything, he still seemed to think he was an imposition. She hoped he wouldn't be such a shadow today. The two of them would get on well, she was certain. Her father was amiable to everyone, after all.

She heard the sound of shuffling bed covers and turned to see that Daniel had been woken by Chantelle's exclamations.

"I'll start on the Christmas breakfast," he said, heaving his body out of bed. "Does your dad like blueberry pancakes?"

"I'm sure he does," Emily told him, wondering whether her father was even able to eat at the moment. He looked so thin.

As Daniel left the room, Emily put her slippers on and wrapped a fluffy bathrobe around her. She went to head downstairs when Chantelle came bounding down the corridor.

"Papa Roy and Terry are already up," she said. "Both their beds are empty."

Emily frowned, confused. It was so early it was still dark outside. But then again, her father was a notorious early riser, and Terry had displayed similar behavior since he'd been staying with them.

Emily took Chantelle's hand and they descended the staircase together. As they went, Emily was delighted to discover that all the Christmas lights had been turned on, providing them with a twinkling path to the living room. There, the first thing she noticed was that the fire was lit -- it's comforting smoky smell permeating the room -- and there was a full breakfast buffet set up on the table by the window. Smiling at them, with mischievous grins, were both Terry and Roy.

"What on earth is going on?" Emily asked, shocked and thrilled by the surprise. "When did you do all this? You must have been up for hours!"

Terry blushed. "I wanted to say thank you for everything you've done for me, so I got up early to make breakfast. I bumped into your father in the kitchen. He'd had the same idea. But it gave me quite a fright, I must admit."

Roy chuckled. "Me too. Emily forgot to tell me there was a guest staying! I thought I'd interrupted Santa collecting his mince pies."

Chantelle laughed hysterically at this. Terry certainly had an air of Santa Claus about him.

"I'm so sorry!" Emily exclaimed, laughing. She felt a little guilty that she'd not thought to mention Terry to her father, but in the shock of his sudden appearance that thought had slipped from her mind entirely.

"Anyway," Roy continued. "Once we'd gotten the introductions out of the way, we decided to get the house all ready for when you woke up. So we made breakfast and I've seen to the plants and chickens. Although, the greenhouse looks like it's in a bit of a sad state."

Chantelle nodded. "The snow was so heavy the roof caved in."

"Then we'll just have to put it all back together again," Roy added.

Chantelle hurried forward and hugged Roy around the middle. Emily smiled at them, touched to see the affection they had for one another, and pleased that Chantelle had her greenhouse buddy back! Then Chantelle hugged Terry.

"Thank you so much for making breakfast," she said.

Terry blushed.

"Well tuck in," Roy said, gesturing to the table, "Before it all goes cold."

They went over to look at all the foodstuffs. There were all different types of eggs, and melon slices, and smoked salmon with cream cheese, and Terry's oatmeal breakfast bars, and small cubes of fried potato, and freshly squeezed orange juice. It reminded Emily of the excessive buffets they'd shared together in Greece. A wonderful sensation of nostalgia overcame her.

Chantelle quickly started piling up her plate.

Just then, the door opened and in walked Daniel. He was holding a tray with a stack of blueberry pancakes on it. He froze at the threshold, looking completely shocked by the room filled with people and food.

"Wait," he said, blinking. "What's going on here?"

Everyone started to laugh. Daniel must have been so tired this morning, he hadn't even noticed the glow of fire light or the fact that all the lights were on!

"Papa Roy and Terry made us breakfast!" Chantelle cried, her mouth full of toast.

"In that case, I guess I'll just add these to the buffet," Daniel shrugged. He came over to the table and squeezed the plate of blueberry pancakes between all the other delights on the table.

Everyone ate, in high spirits and filled with Christmas cheer.

"Did we tell you about the silver, Papa Roy?" Chantelle asked over her second plate of food.

Roy looked intrigued. "No, what silver?"

"Trevor had it all in his secret cellar," she explained. "Terry helped us find it so we're going to share the money from selling it."

Terry shook his head. "I keep trying to tell them no. I couldn't accept a gift of that magnitude."

Roy turned his attention to Emily. "How much silver are we talking, darling?"

Emily didn't want to discuss money at the table, especially when she hadn't yet told Terry how much his share would come to. "Let's just say it's a complete collection of William Gamble kitchenware."

She knew her father, as a keen antiquarian, would understand what that really meant. By the way his eyes widened, she knew he had worked it out.

"That's... quite the find," he replied. "Did Trevor tell you it was there? I knew he loved collecting old pieces like that but I had no idea it was to such an extent!"

"He never said a word," Emily replied. "The closest he came was alluding to it in his will, which stated that his home and any items found on the grounds of his property was to go to us. I thought he was just being specific in case some distant relative appeared and tried to find a loophole in order to claim things off him." She sipped her decaf coffee. "But I expect it was a little hint."

Roy started to chuckle then. "It looks like your old man must have worn off on him over the years after all! I used to tell Trevor about my secret hiding places, about how I'd built a new secret tunnel or staircase, about the hollowed out bricks I'd filled with treasure. He always used to scoff at me, saying I was ridiculous. I don't even think he believed me half the time. But looks like he took a leaf out of my book after all!"

"Are there any more secret places in this house?" Chantelle asked Roy.

Roy just tapped his nose. "This house has more secrets than even I know," was all he would tell her.

They finished eating their food and cleared up the mess together, making the chores more enjoyable with a backing track of festive music blaring through the inn's speakers. Once everything was tidy, Chantelle declared that it was time for presents. They all went to leave the kitchen, and Emily noticed Terry holding back.

"I ought to give you a bit of family time," he said to Emily.

Chantelle must have overheard, because she turned around and grasped Terry by the elbow of his sweater.

"Come on, Terry!" she exclaimed. "You're family too, now. Don't you get it?"

Emily saw the way he fought back his tears of gratitude as he allowed Chantelle to lead him through the corridor into the living room, before depositing him on the couch.

"We have presents for you too," she explained.

Chantelle went to the tree and found all of the parcels that had sweaters in them from the tree lighting festival. She handed them around to everyone.

They all opened their gifts at the same time. Roy and Terry -- the only people there who didn't know what was inside -- unfolded their sweaters and laughed wholeheartedly as they held them up to inspect them.

"Oh my!" Roy cried, looking at the sparkly reindeer face. He put it on straight away. Though it swamped his tiny frame, he looked very pleased with himself.

"Come on Terry!" Chantelle coaxed, after she had put her own sweater on. "Everyone has to wear one!"

She gestured to Emily and Daniel who, having already unwrapped their sweaters, were pulling them on over their heads.

"See," Chantelle said. "You have to put it on so we're all matching!"

Finally, Terry got into the spirit of things, and put his garish outfit on, much to Chantelle's delight.

"I wonder if Stu, Clyde and Evan have opened theirs yet?" Daniel laughed as he slid his own on.

Emily remembered the elf ones they'd bought for them.

"I doubt they're awake yet," Emily said with a chuckle. "No one without children wakes up this early on Christmas. They'll all still be in their beds sleeping soundly."

"I wish they'd stayed here," Chantelle said.

"They wanted to be with their own families on Christmas," Emily explained.

"Nana Patty isn't with her family," Chantelle refuted.

Emily couldn't argue with that. Though she hadn't expected Patricia to come for Christmas, a little part of her had hoped that she might.

"Neither is Cassie," Chantelle continued, referring to Daniel's mom.

Daniel looked a little glum at the mention of his estranged family.

"Let's open the rest of the gifts," Emily said suddenly, wanting to cheer everyone up.

"Good idea," Daniel said, clearly grateful to have a distraction.

He went and sat beside the tree, handing gift after gift out to Chantelle. She read each of the tags aloud and, unsurprisingly, the vast majority of them were for her. She opened up all of her beautifully wrapped gifts, exclaiming in delight at a silky party dress, a tin of coloring pencils, a box set of books.

"Did Santa bring anything for us?" Daniel joked as the presents piled up around her.

"Of course he did!" Chantelle exclaimed.

She crawled under the tree and emerged with two crazily-wrapped gifts. They had all the hallmarks of Chantelle's own hand; mismatched neon paper, ribbons, glitter, stickers. Emily took hers, feeling extremely grateful that she had such a sweet daughter who would think to get her a present.

She peeled the paper off carefully, and saw that Chantelle had made her a picture frame. It had space for five photographs and in each of the gaps Chantelle had written a name: Daddy, Chantelle, Charlotte, Papa Roy, Nana Patty. On the top it said *FAMILY* and there were found objects stuck all around the edges; acorns, pebbles from the beach, a piece of driftwood from the island.

Emily clutched it to her chest. "Oh Chantelle, I love it," she exclaimed.

It truly was a touching gift, and Emily felt so blessed to have such a wonderful family around her.

After all the gifts were opened, the family decided to go on a gentle stroll, taking the dogs with them. Emily directed them through the forests outside the back of the house in order to show them all the house that Amy was in the process of purchasing. Then they headed down to the ocean front, walking around the side of the harbor to the woodshop that Daniel was buying. Finally, they headed home via the main street where the Christmas tree was, so that Roy could see it.

The walk ended up taking much longer than Emily had anticipated. By the time they got home it was already well past midday.

"We'd better get cooking," she exclaimed. "All hands on deck!"

Everyone helped out in the kitchen, cooking all the different dishes for their Christmas dinner. Terry knew some interesting recipes for the vegetables, showing Chantelle how to make braised spiced cabbage with apple pieces. Daniel took charge of the turkey, whilst Roy mulled the wine, and Emily focused on the roast potatoes. Somehow between them all, they managed to create a Christmas meal without any disasters!

They all sat down in the dining room to eat, laughing and joking their way through the meal. Emily realized as she looked around that it had indeed been the best Christmas ever.

CHAPTER FIFTEEN

"What do you think about my new clock?" Chantelle asked Roy over breakfast the next morning.

Emily watched as her father examined Chantelle's most recent project.

"It looks marvellous," he said, finally. "I'm very impressed. You've chosen quite an ambitious design."

"I wanted to try something a bit tricker," Chantelle told him. "Now that I know how to make a standard clock, I wanted to see if I could do one more like you would, with carved parts that show the inner workings."

Roy looked thoroughly impressed. "Well, you're certainly doing that."

He sat beside her and they began sifting through cogs and bolts, searching for the best ones. It filled Emily's heart with love to see them working together.

"Are we going to do more work on the greenhouse today?" Chantelle asked after a little while.

"Try not to tire Papa Roy too much," Emily told her.

"I don't mind at all," Roy replied. "I'd like to see the greenhouse back to its former glory before I leave."

At the mention of leaving, Emily felt a swirl of nausea in her belly. In all the excitement of Roy's visit and Christmas, she'd not even thought to ask how long he'd been planning on staying with them. "When are you leaving?" she asked.

"My flight home is on New Year's Day. I wanted to stay long enough to spend a bit of time with Charlotte." He squeezed Chantelle's shoulders then. "And this one, of course."

Emily felt a little relieved to know they still had some days to enjoy one another's company, but she knew that when the time came for her father to leave it would break her heart.

"Will you come back again another time?" Chantelle asked.

Roy fell silent then. When he spoke, it was slowly and carefully, as though he were taking pains to chose the most diplomatic words possible. "Darling, there won't be another time. There won't be another chance." He tapped the clock on the table. "I'm like a broken old clock that can't be wound. There's not much tick left in me."

125

"Can't we fix you?" Chantelle asked, tears welling in his eyes.

Roy shook his head, sadly. "Not this time. And that's okay. It's my time to pass."

"Will you go to the warm, happy place where auntie Charlotte went?" Chantelle asked.

Roy smiled then and ruffled her hair. "I will. Like Charlotte, I'll be watching you. I'll be there as you grow up. I'll see all your school plays. I'll be there when you graduate. There when you get married. When you win the Nobel Prize."

Chantelle started to laugh then, amused by his imagined future for her. She was clearly comforted by his words, even if she was still filled with sorrow about this being his last visit to Sunset Harbor. Emily was too. She didn't want this to be the last time she saw her beloved father.

Daniel and Terry entered the kitchen then, back from walking the dogs.

"Who's ready to work on the greenhouse?" he asked.

Chantelle leapt up, her arm straight in the air. "ME!"

Roy stood too. "And me."

They all looked at Emily, still seated at the kitchen table.

"I hope you all don't mind, but I have a few things to sort out today. Business things. And I'm so tired, I think I need a nap."

Daniel came over and kissed her head. "Do whatever you need to, darling."

It felt so good to have him back to his caring self. Christmas had brought them all closer together.

Emily watched her family bundle out of the back door before heading upstairs and getting into bed.

She started by looking over Bryony's winter marketing plans, the ones she'd drawn up whilst Emily was stuck in hospital. In typical Bryony fashion her proposals were all incredibly creative, well thought through, and extensively researched. But amongst the myriad of ideas, one thing stood out to Emily most of all. A winter-themed New Year's Eve ball.

They'd thrown parties at the inn before, but the idea of a ball really struck Emily. They'd not done anything like that before! In the whole time she'd lived in Sunset Harbor she'd not known of anything like it. It seemed like a fun and unique way to bring in a bit of winter income, not to mention a wonderful send off for her father.

She left her room, searching for Daniel. She found him, Roy, Chantelle and Terry in the greenhouse, working hard to fix it.

"How do you guys feel about holding a winter ball?" she asked.

Chantelle seemed thrilled. "When?"

"New Year's Eve."

"That doesn't leave much time to plan," Daniel said.

"I know, but we can do it," Emily said.

"What about the baby?" Daniel said. "She'll be born by then. How will you organize a party whilst caring for a newborn?"

Emily shrugged. "It won't change a thing. I'll just organize everything from my bed between breast feeds!"

"I think it's a great idea," Roy said supportively. "There's nothing too ambitious for my daughter. Think big, darling. Reach for the stars."

"We can all chip in to help," Terry added. "If you need a rest, you've got all of us around you to take some of the slack."

"See," Emily added, grinning at Daniel.

"I'll change diapers," Chantelle said.

"So will I," Roy added.

Terry joined in. "I'll do laundry. Make dinner. You know I hate to be idle."

Daniel shook his head, realizing there was no way to refute Emily. She'd set her mind to it and there was no way he was going to change it.

"Fine," he said, eventually. "Let's have a New Year's Eve ball."

Everyone cheered.

CHAPTER SIXTEEN

The next day, Emily threw herself into preparing for the New Year's party. The final town meeting to approve Raven's inn was tomorrow, and she wanted to make the announcement there, knowing everyone in town would be in attendance, and that it may be just the way to soften the blow of the announcement. It would certainly send a clear signal to Raven that Emily was going to fight for her business, that she wasn't going to lie down and let Raven bulldoze her way through Sunset Harbor!

There wasn't much time to organize the event, so Emily got straight on the phone. First, she called Amy and asked for her help. Of course, her friend jumped at the opportunity. Then she called Roman and asked whether he'd be interested in playing a set at the ball.

"For your usual fee, of course," she told him. "I'm not asking you to play for free!"

"I'd love to do it!" he exclaimed. "But instead of paying me, can you donate the fee to my charity? It's a local Maine charity that provides support to the parents of premature babies. All the funds from my Christmas single are going to them as well."

"That's a lovely idea," Emily agreed, casting her mind back to the sight of the preemie ward and all the tiny babies in their incubators under purple UV lights. Seeing them had tugged at her heart-strings, and she'd felt so awful for the parents going through such anguish. "You know what, I'm going to match your fee donation with an equal sum from the sale of the tickets. We can also have collection buckets in case anyone wants to donate any spare cash on the night."

Agreeing that the ball would be the perfect opportunity to raise awareness and extra funds for the premature babies charity, Emily ended the call and next went about speaking to Parker regarding catering the events. He was relieved to have the work and agreed in a second. Raj, the next call she made, was thrilled to provide white flowers and trees for the event and the Elves cleaning company took on the cleaning contract. Everything quickly started falling into place.

The best thing with all the organizing was that Emily could distract herself from the fact that today she was exactly 42 weeks pregnant. Tomorrow morning she was seeing Doctor Arkwright to discuss being induced, something she'd promised the doctor and Daniel she'd consider at 42 weeks even though she really didn't want to do it at all. It also would be the beginning to her daily check ins with the doctor, the frequent monitoring, the inevitable disapproving looks from her friends and family as she continued to refuse medical advice and go against being chemically induced. The warnings about carrying on her pregnancy beyond this date echoed in her mind.

Emily realized then that she did have one ally. A very unlikely one, in fact. And that was her mother.

She decided to call her.

"Are you in labor?" Patricia asked.

"No. Not yet," Emily told her. "That's actually why I'm calling."

"Oh?"

"Today is week 42."

"And?"

Patricia was being typically blunt.

"And, I know I'm going to start getting pressured to be induced," she said. "Daniel wants me to. So does my doctor."

"Oh, pft," Patricia replied. "Ignore them all, darling. You know what's best. I've told you a million times that you were late and Charlotte was late, so our babies clearly just take a little longer to grow. Trust your own instincts."

Emily felt greatly comforted. "Thanks mom," she said.

There was a long moment of silence as neither said anything. Emily was half expecting her mom to say goodbye and end the call, but instead she said, "How was your Christmas day?"

Emily blinked in surprise. It wasn't often her mother took an interest in her life.

"It was wonderful actually," Emily told her. "Dad's here."

"He is?" Patricia asked, and the shock in her voice was audible.

"I know. I didn't think he'd come. But after my hospital scare he realized he wanted to spend Christmas with us."

"How long is he staying for?" Patricia asked.

"Until New Year's Day," Emily told her. "He's promised Chantelle he'll help fix up the greenhouse and we're having a New Year's Eve ball here so he's staying for that as well." She paused then, a small glimmer of a thought sparking in her mind. "I don't suppose you'd want to come to the ball as well, would you?"

Patricia had been giving off certain vibes recently, Emily thought, about wanting to reconcile with Roy before he passed.

There was a lot of unfinished business between them, and it had only been since Emily had announced his illness that Patricia had seemed to even be able to consider the prospect of burying the hatchet. Their relationship had improved greatly over the last few months and Emily wondered whether her mom might also want to patch things up with Roy.

"A ball?" Patricia asked, sounding a little snooty. "Goodness, do you think I don't have anything better to do on New Year's than attend a small town ball? Darling, I live in New York City! I have appearances to keep."

Emily rolled her eyes, but she wasn't offended. For the first time in their relationship she could tell that Patricia's behavior was just a shield, that her abrupt tone and dismissiveness was her way of protecting herself from the pain of reality, from accepting the truth that Roy would not be with them much longer.

"Just think about it," Emily said. "Chantelle would love to see you."

There was hesitation on the other end of the line. Finally, Patricia spoke. "And I her."

Emily smiled, knowing her mom was secretly touched.

"Now, I must go," Patricia said, hurriedly. "Call me when you go into labor. And remember what I said. YOU are the boss, Emily. YOU and only YOU know what is best for your body and your baby. Don't let anyone make you do something you don't want to."

"Thanks, mom," Emily said.

It was the best advice she'd ever gotten from the woman, and Emily cherished it.

She finished up organizing some more things for the New Year's ball -- speaking to the printing company who'd be making the rush order of posters and flyers for the event, organizing the fireworks display that would take place in the grounds of the inn, and finally putting in a huge order with her liquor company. When she'd done as much as she could handle, she put her mental energy into the two big events of tomorrow; the town meeting that would decide the fate of Raven Kingsley's inn, and her appointment with Doctor Arkwright.

Amy had been livid last time at her refusal to bash Raven's inn. Maybe she should just give in and say what everyone wanted her to, what she herself knew would be the easiest option. But Patricia's advice rang in her mind. Don't let anyone make you do something you don't want to. It was going to be her motto for tomorrow, words that would get her through both the doctor's appointment and the town meeting. At least, she hoped as much.

CHAPTER SEVENTEEN

"Good morning Emily," Rose Arkwright said as she welcomed Emily and Daniel into her office. "Please, take a seat."

They did, and the doctor sat at her desk.

"We're here," she smiled. "Week 42! From now on, we'll say you're 42 + however many days. So right now, you're 42 + 1."

Emily nodded her understanding.

"How do you feel?" Doctor Arkwright asked. "Uncomfortable?"

"The same as I was before," Emily replied. "There's not been much of a change. I'm not sick of the pregnancy at all."

"Are you ready to book in an induction date?"

Emily hesitated. She tried to hold onto her mom's steely resolve and not falter under the pressure. She swallowed hard.

"No," she said. "Not yet."

Daniel exhaled loudly.

"You don't approve of this decision?" the doctor asked him.

"I don't," Daniel admitted. He addressed Emily. "I don't know what you're waiting for. Wouldn't now be the perfect time for Charlotte to be born, while your father is here and alive to meet her?"

Emily winced. Her father's impending death was a cruel thing to bring into it. Even Doctor Arkwright seemed shocked by his comment. She turned her gaze away. Emily felt embarrassed that all their dirty laundry was being aired in front of her, that she'd been forced into the role of marriage counsellor as well as doctor.

"We've discussed this," Emily told him, her cheeks growing red. "I already explained to you that I didn't want to be induced."

"I thought you were open to it," came Daniel's rebuke. "That you might change your mind."

"You mean you thought I'd be weak and give in to your demands if you kept pushing?" Emily snapped.

She folded her arms. In her peripheral vision she could see Doctor Arkwright turning her chair away to give them some privacy and she felt deeply embarrassed to have a witness during this spat.

"You keep making it sound like I'm out to get you," Daniel refuted, the tips of his ears turning pink with suppressed anger. "I want what's best for you. I only say these things because I'm worried. You said you'd have a membrane sweep after Christmas and book in for an induction. I'm not making it up. It's what you told me. Is it because of the party now that you're wanting to delay it again?"

Emily's mouth dropped open. "Don't be so ludicrous. Of course it isn't! I'm not trying to make childbirth fit in with my schedule. I'm hurt you'd even suggest such a thing."

"I'm just trying to understand," Daniel said. His voice sounded less angry now, more desperate and confused. "You said you'd book a date and now you're going back on it."

Emily didn't know what she could tell him to make him understand.

"I'm sorry, Daniel," she said finally, her gaze turning downwards. "I just said that because I was trying to accomodate you. I didn't think it would come this far, honestly. I thought she'd be here by now. But the longer it goes on the more certain I am. I've made up my mind. This is what I want."

Daniel cast an appealing gaze towards the doctor. But she remained neutral. There was nothing she could do, anyway. No one could force Emily to have her baby.

"Why don't we do our checks?" the doctor said. "And make sure we've got a good eye on everything. And agree to keep open minds. You might feel different tomorrow."

Emily nodded, to placate them both more than anything. But she knew in her heart what she wanted. No one was going to talk her out of it.

*

As soon as the appointment was over, Daniel drove them to the town meeting, the short journey there taking place in frosty silence.

When Emily entered the town hall, she noticed that people were looking at her warily, like it was her fault that the inevitable approval was soon to be announced. It was the last thing she needed right now, to feel that more people were against her, to be confronted with even more disappointed faces.

She faltered, hanging back by the door, not wanting to join any of her friends. Amy and Harry were only a short distance away but Emily stayed right where she was, as if she'd planted roots in the ground.

Mayor Hansen took to the podium and the general hubbub of chatter died down. He banged his gavel, commanding absolute silence. The whole room held its breath.

"Well, the town has spoken," he began. "Which leaves it to me to announce the outcome." He paused and swallowed and directed his next statement to Raven. "The town has rejected the new inn. I'm so sorry."

There was a huge eruption of noise, mainly gasps of shock. No one had been expecting that result! But the surprise soon turned to elation, as the contingent that had voted against the inn started to celebrate the result.

Raven Kingsley just looked stunned. She blinked at Mayor Hansen who, even from this distance, Emily could tell was offering his sincere condolences.

"Thank goodness," Daniel said beside Emily, leaning towards her ear. "That *is* a relief."

But Emily could focus only on Raven, on her crushed expression. She felt so bad for the woman. It would be wrong to celebrate her misfortune. She couldn't help but feel disappointed with her friends for the way they were behaving.

"I need to speak to her," she told Daniel, moving to head towards of the hall.

He took her arm, stopping her in her tracks. "Why?" he asked, frowning deeply.

"I just do," Emily said, shaking herself free of him.

She didn't wait for his reaction, instead heading straight through the crowds to where Raven was sitting. She was bent forward, her face buried in her hands, her glossy black hair obscuring her features like a widow's veil.

"I'm so sorry, Raven," Emily said. "I can only begin to imagine how this must feel right now."

To her surprise, when Raven looked up and saw who it was standing over her, she burst into tears. Emily had always thought of the woman as cold and emotionless. Seeing her vulnerability tugged at Emily's heart strings. Instinctively, she crouched down and wrapped her arms around Raven.

"Come on," she said in a kind, soothing voice. "Why don't we go somewhere a bit quieter to talk? Get away from this crowd." She cast accusational eyes around the room at the people who were gawping at them.

Raven nodded and stood, keeping her head bowed as she collected her crocodile-skin purse. As she led the way, Emily felt like she was security helping a disgraced star flee the paparazzi. People jostled and whispered as the two of them headed towards the main exit of the town hall.

When they reached the door, Emily was confronted by Daniel standing Amy and Harry. They were all glaring at her.

"Raven and I are just going to have a quick chat," she told them. "At Joe's. I won't be long."

Daniel looked exasperated, like this was yet another betrayal. First she wouldn't agree to be induced and now she was rubbing shoulders with the enemy. Emily felt awful for it, but had to stay true to herself. She couldn't abandon Raven in her time of need.

Amy turned to Daniel then. "Why don't you come back to ours for a bit?" she said. "We could do with a catch up. It's been too long."

Emily knew that all three would use the opportunity to vent about her; Daniel for her willfulness over the pregnancy, Amy over her perceived betrayal by siding with Raven, and Harry for all the drama her decisions were causing. It didn't seem to matter to them that they'd got the outcome they wanted, just that Emily had not been on their side when it counted.

"Sure," Daniel replied, testily. "Thanks." He handed his truck keys to Emily. "You okay to drive yourself home?"

"Of course," she said, snatching them out of his hand. "I'm pregnant not dying."

She didn't look back to see their reactions as she hurried out of the door.

Despite the bitingly cold wind, it was a relief to be out of that claustrophobic place and out into the open air.

"Why are you being so kind to me?" Raven said through her tears as they descended the stone steps leading from the town hall. "No one else is."

"Because I've been where you are," Emily explained. "I know how awful it can be to feel like the town is against you. And as much as I love this place and the people in it, going against the grain can be quite intimidating." They reached the bottom and began to walk along the sidewalk heading for Joe's Diner. "Besides, we both share the same dream. And I know how I would feel if it had been snatched away from me at the last minute."

Raven seemed too miserable to even reply. They finished the rest of the short walk in silence then went inside the diner, making the bell above the door tinkle.

Joe looked up from behind the counter. Emily noted his surprised expression as he watched the two of them -- two rivals -- taking a seat together in one of the booths. He came over then, coffee pot in hand and a confused expression on his face.

"How did the meeting go?" he asked Emily. But he must have noticed the way that Raven was weeping bitterly then and put two and two together in his mind. "Sorry, stupid question," he added under his breath.

He poured them both coffee -- decaf for Emily of course -- then hovered beside them as if he had more to say. Joe was known for his nosiness, and Emily usually just thought of it as a harmless foible. But now wasn't the time. She shot him a slightly stern look and he retreated back to the counter. Finally they had some privacy.

Raven pulled some tissues from the dispenser beside them and wiped her nose.

"Thank you, Emily," she said. "You know you're one of the few people in this town who hasn't bashed me."

"I know," Emily said sadly. "This town can be suspicious of outsiders. I can only apologize."

"Don't," Raven refuted. "They were right to be. I'm everything they said I was."

Emily frowned. "What do you mean?"

Raven took a deep breath like she was about to divulge some deep, dark secret.

"I mean they were right about my plans for the hotel. Everyone was scared that I would ruin this town with a big, ugly corporate building made of glass. That I would have rented out the rooms at a loss just to drive other's out of business. And they were right. It's what I would have done. It's what I always do."

Emily was shocked by the revelation. "But I thought you wanted to settle here," she stammered. "Start a new life. Turn over a new leaf. That's what you told me and I... I fought for you, Raven."

She felt hurt, like Raven had taken advantage of her kindness. She'd put a lot on the line by supporting her and now it looked like she'd made the wrong judgement after all.

"Honestly, I don't know what I want anymore," Raven said, blowing her nose again. "Ever since the divorce my mind's been all over the place. You know, I got into this business with my ex-husband? It's his thing, really. I never stopped to think whether I wanted it for myself or not. I have a degree in Political Science, for God's sake! Running a hotel chain was clearly not part of the plan." She laughed, bitterly.

"Why are you telling me this, Raven?" Emily asked. She was still hurt about the shocking revelation that Raven would have run her out of business given half the chance.

"Because I want you to know it wasn't personal, okay? After he left me I was so focused on proving myself, showing I could do

135

it without him. It made me colder, more ruthless. Then you were there with your kindness and your compassion and I guess…" She sighed, like it pained her to admit it. "I guess I realized that I didn't *want* to crush you."

Emily raised an eyebrow. Did that count as a compliment in Raven's world? "Um… thanks, I guess," she said.

"I mean that I didn't want the inn anymore," Raven said, trying to explain her somewhat tactless comment. "Because I knew what it would mean for you and your family. For your town. I was done fighting and competing and trying to prove myself to some idiot man whose priorities are all wrong anyway so I…" She paused again, swallowing hard. "I voted against myself."

Emily couldn't believe what she was hearing. "You rigged the vote to lose?"

"Pretty much," Raven replied. "I mean, withdrawing would have been a PR disaster, but losing I can spin to my advantage somehow. Blame it on the small town mentality."

Emily just blinked in surprise. She couldn't believe that Raven had chosen her to confide in. She must be so lonely looking down at them all from her ivory tower if the only person she could spill her guts to was her rival.

"Well, I suppose I appreciate you not wanting to destroy me," Emily told her. "But what will you do now?"

"I'm leaving town," Raven said. "The kids hate it here. There's not even enough space at Mallory's to send Laverne there. It's not fair she has to go to public school."

Emily bit her lip, choosing not to take offence to Raven's implication that the public school Chantelle attended was somehow providing an inferior education.

"But what about the building?" Emily asked her.

"I'll sell it on," Raven said blankly.

"But how?" Emily asked. "You'll never find a buyer. I mean, the zoning board have been sitting on that place for years. Decades even. Not even Trevor Mann could get the wheels turning on that place! What makes you think you'll be able to sell it?"

Raven looked distraught. "I had no idea. You mean to say I'm stuck with it? Here? In this place?"

Emily managed to keep her composure, in spite of all of Raven's barbed insults.

"What am I supposed to do now?" Raven wailed.

A sudden thought came into Emily's mind. From her mom's uncompromising attitude to her dad's faith in her and encouragement she should aim for the stars, Emily suddenly found herself coming up with a crazy plan.

"Sell it to me," Emily said.

Raven's eyes widened. "What?"

"Sell it to me," Emily repeated. "It's your only option. The only person who'll want to buy that place is a local, and the only one with the impetus is me. It makes sense. Otherwise you'll either have to live there or abandon it and cut your losses."

Emily thought of the miracle silverware in Trevor's cellar she could use as a down payment. And then there was the fact that Trevor had always loved that oceanfront property. Suddenly, it seemed to all be coming together. It made perfect sense. She could honor Trevor by restoring the grand oceanfront property like he'd always wanted, and at the same time give Raven a get out of jail free card. Everyone would win.

"So?" Emily pressed. "What do you say?"

"Don't you need to consult with your husband about that?" Raven asked warily.

"He'll agree," Emily said. "I mean, we just put on offer in to buy him a shop so he can hardly argue against me buying a house! I can go and speak to him right now," she added. "Call you once I've convinced him." She winked.

Feeling buoyant for the first time that day, Emily bade farewell to Raven. She'd felt certain fate had something special in store for her and now it was all starting to make sense. From the hospital scare bringing her father to her, to the discovery of Trevor's silver bringing her the possibility of restoring the property he'd always adored, it seemed as if the stars were starting to align for Emily.

CHAPTER EIGHTEEN

Emily felt exhausted by the time she returned home in Daniel's truck. It would have been a trying day even if she hadn't been heavily pregnant and overly emotional from hormones. But it was the whole bizarre situation with Raven that really tipped it over the edge!

When she got out of the truck, she immediately noticed that the garage door was open and Daniel's bike was gone. Of course he'd go out on one of his sulking motorcycle rides, Emily thought. She shouldn't really expect any different from him.

Irritated, she headed inside the inn and listened out for the sounds of the others. It was completely quiet which meant only one thing; everyone would be out in the greenhouses. She walked through the corridor and exited through the backdoor in the kitchen, crossing over the lawn to the side that had once belonged to Trevor.

From the outside, the greenhouse was looking amazing now. George had helped them pick a better type of glass and different fixtures for the structure that would be more sturdy should it snow heavily again in the future. If anything, this greenhouse looked bigger and grander than the last one, reminding Emily of an old Victorian orangery. In fact, it would look very fitting with the Queen Anne style manor house she was in the process of purchasing off Raven!

She stepped inside to the sounds of chatter and hammering.

"There you are," she said, passing by a cluster of large bushy green plants in pots that were waiting to be planted, to see Chantelle, Roy and Terry hard at work.

"Emily-Jane," Roy said. He raised his eyebrows. "What happened at the town meeting?"

"You won't believe it," Emily said. "Raven's plans were rejected."

"That's good news, isn't it?" Chantelle asked.

"Yes, but she seemed devastated," Emily said. "We had a coffee and she told me all about how bad a decision it was coming here, what with her divorce. Then she dropped a bombshell on me. She wants to sell up and leave Sunset Harbor."

Roy looked surprised. "But she'll never get a buyer," he said. "That place was hard to shift twenty years ago. It'll only get worse.

138

No one in their right mind would want to take on a project like that!"

Emily bit her lip.

"You need a house," Chantelle said to Terry. "Why don't you buy it?"

Terry began to laugh. "I need a *house,* my dear, not a decaying mansion! And beside, where would I grow the Christmas trees?" His chuckles started up again. "Honestly, the only person who'd purchase that place off Raven would be a lunatic."

Emily run her hands. But there was no hiding it now. They may as well know the truth.

"I guess you should call me a lunatic then," she said. "Not in my right mind. Because I offered to take it off her hands."

Everyone froze and stared at her.

"You're buying the house?" Roy asked.

She nodded. "Yup. That decaying mansion might soon be mine. Once I've run it past Daniel, that is." She tried not to think of the incredulous expression he give her when she broke the news.

Emily realized as she spoke that if she indeed got the go-ahead from Daniel, this would be the first house she'd ever bought for herself. The inn had been gifted to her by her father. Trevor's house came to her via his will as inheritance. But this was the first time she'd ever bought a home on her own accord. Even if it was a ruin, purchasing it would be a significant milestone.

"I thought I could fund it through the sale of the silver," she explained, feeling more confident in her decision and less like she'd just made the craziest mistake of her life. "Find a way to restore it, just like Trevor always wanted."

Roy's stunned expression softened then. "That's a lovely idea."

Terry blushed. "I suppose the only person who'd *not* be a lunatic to buy it would be a local who wanted to preserve the history of the place..." He trailed off.

Chantelle grinned at Emily. "I love that plan, mommy. But what does Daddy think?"

"I'm not sure," Emily confessed. "He's kind of mad at me right now."

"Oh no," Chantelle said, looking sad. "Are you still arguing?"

Roy approached Emily then. "Perhaps we ought to go inside and have some cocoa?" he said in a soft voice. "I'm sure Chantelle doesn't want to hear this."

Emily nodded. He was right. Chantelle shouldn't be given a spectators seat to her parent's drama.

Roy took her by the shoulder and called out behind him. "We won't be a minute! You carry on with that planting, sweetheart."

They headed in to the kitchen.

"So what's going on with Daniel?" Roy asked.

Emily sat heavily at the table and dropped her head in her hands. "It's baby stuff. he wants me to be induced but I don't want to. Then at the meeting I went off with Raven because she was upset and he looked betrayed. When I got home I saw he'd gone off on his bike which is a big flashing neon sign that he's mad at me."

Roy listened quietly, making the cocoa as she spoke.

"I doubt he'll be best pleased when he gets home and finds out you're planning on buying another house," he said when she was done, glancing over his shoulder at her slumped form.

"Ohhhhh…" Emily wailed. "Don't remind me. That was a dumb decision, huh?"

Roy came over with the mugs steaming cocoa and placed one in front of her. He sat in the seat opposite.

"Actually, I think it's a really smart idea."

"You do?"

"Yes. You're helping someone in need for starters. Secondly, wasn't half the reason people were mad at you at the meeting because they didn't want an outsider to come in and ruin the look of the town? Whatever you choose to do with the place it will at least be in keeping with the look of the town. And then the final thing, which is a little more selfish. You'll be buying the only other property in town that currently has zoning board approval for an inn. You'll be effectively eliminating future competition. If you wanted to start a new inn beside the ocean you could. The town wouldn't vote against you. You know that."

Emily looked at her father, surprised that what he was telling her was true. It was only because the town didn't want Raven Kingsley to open a hotel that they'd voted her down in the meeting. The zoning board had already given a green light to the project. If she were to put in a proposal to restore the building rather than tear it down, and open a new inn that fit Sunset Harbor like a glove, they'd probably rally around to support her.

But then she remembered how badly things were going at the inn this winter. If she couldn't make a success of her one location, what made her think she'd do any better with a second?

Emily looked up at her father. He was always such a supportive person, someone she felt at ease confiding in.

"What if I fail?" she said, allowing her deepest fears to the surface. "I mean the inn's not made any income so far this winter.

I've even had to cut my staff member's shifts down. My business might fail as it is. Daniel has his woodshop to focus on so he won't be around to help, so whatever I do I'll be doing on my own. With a baby. Wouldn't a whole new place be a case of biting off more than I can chew?"

"It sounds like you're trying to talk yourself out of it," Roy said, kindly.

Emily shrugged. "Maybe I am."

"But…" Roy prompted.

Emily smirked. Her father knew her so well he could tell there was more on the tip of her tongue.

"But, is it bad that I really *really* want to try? Am I allowed to just be greedy for once and want something and then have it just because?"

Roy frowned. "Is that a rhetorical question?"

Emily shook her head. Roy chuckled.

"In which case," he said, "No, it's not bad to have something just because you want it. But something that big should probably be a joint decision with your husband, don't you think?"

As if on cue, Emily heard the sound of Daniel's motorcycle approaching the inn along the drive. A little surge of panic rose in her as she realized she was going to have to admit what she'd done. He was going to be pissed.

She braced herself, waiting for him to enter the inn. A few moments later, she heard the door slam.

"We're in here," she called over her shoulder.

There were footsteps, and then Daniel appeared in the doorway, crash helmet in hand. He looked immediately suspicious.

"What's going on?" he asked.

"Let me make you a cocoa," Roy said, standing up.

"I'm good thanks," Daniel told him, gesturing for him to remain seated with an outstretched hand. "Emily? What's going on? You look guilty."

"Did you have a nice ride?" she asked, avoiding confronting the real question and dealing with the inevitable fall out.

"*Emily…*" Daniel said sternly.

Emily took a breath. "Okay. Promise me you won't be mad."

Daniel rolled his eyes. "How can I tell that I'm already going to hate this?" He sat down beside her, placing his helmet on the table, and looked at her expectantly. "I'm not promising anything so you may as well just tell me what you've done."

"I sort of maybe promised someone I'd buy their house," Emily said, wincing as she spoke.

He paused. Blinked. "You..."

"It's Raven's. She wants to get out of Sunset Harbor and you know no one sane would pay money for that house and I thought it would benefit everyone it I just bought it off her. That way she can leave and I can find a way to save the house rather than replace it with something cheap and ugly. I know, I know, the house is structurally unsound at the moment but I thought it would be a nice way to honor Trevor as well..."

She was rambling a mile a minute, and running out of breath fast. As she spoke, Daniel's eyes were growing wider and wider. But not with anger, she realized, but with delight.

Suddenly, he took her by the shoulders, his face breaking out into a wide grin.

"This is amazing!" he cried.

Now it was Emily's turn to look suspicious. "Wait. What? Why aren't you mad?"

"Mad?" Daniel cried. "Why *would* I be mad? I'm thrilled!"

He bundled her into his arms. The shock of his reaction made Emily feel numb all over. She couldn't process what was happening. Finally he let her go and held both her hands in his across the table.

"Daniel, did you fall off your bike and get a concussion?" Emily asked in all seriousness.

Daniel just laughed. He looked over at Roy. "You haven't told her the story, have you?"

Roy shook his head. Emily noticed he was smiling, too. She looked back at Daniel.

"What story?"

Daniel's hands tightened on hers. He gazed into her eyes as he spoke.

"You remember how I told you about hiding here as a kid, in your dad's shed, and how he encouraged me to get my life back on track?"

"Of course," Emily replied.

"Well, one time we were walking along the harbor after a fishing trip and he asked me to try to imagine my future, how I wanted it to look if everything went my way. He asked me to describe what I saw. Well, we were standing there in front of that house, and I told him that one day I'd own it and live there with a family who loved me."

Emily felt emotion catch in the back of her throat. "You never told me..." she stammered.

142

"I never needed to," he said. "Most of it came true anyway with this place. But to know that…" His eyes misted over then. "That the future Roy made me imagine has come true." He stopped, wiped his tears, overcome suddenly with emotion.

"Oh Daniel," Emily said. She reached for him, wrapping him in her arms. He let out a hiccuping sob onto her shoulder. "So you're not mad?"

"I'm not mad," he replied in her ear.

"And you think it's a good idea?"

"I think it's the best idea."

"And you've forgiven me for not wanting to be induced?"

He drew back then and looked at her with a sideways smirk. With a light-hearted voice, he said, "Don't push your luck, Mrs Morey.".

CHAPTER NINETEEN

After her doctor's appointment the next morning, (all healthy at 42 + 2!) Emily and Daniel met Roy and Chantelle outside of Raven's ocean front building.

The building was covered in scaffolding which Raven had had put in place to secure things, but its exterior still looked stunning and unique. Arcitecutarlly it was in the Queen Anne style, clearly Victorian in era, and looked like it may well have been the first building in the whole town. No wonder Trevor wanted to turn it into a museum. The place oozed history.

"Why does it look so crazy?" Chantelle asked, peering up at the asymmetrical facade, the overhanging eaves and the almost Shakespearean looking balustrades.

"Because it's completely unique," Emily told her. "Look, even its towers are polygonal!"

Chantelle giggled. "It looks like my dolls house but giant sized."

"Everyone put on a hard hat," Daniel explained. "And be extremely careful inside. No running, Chantelle."

"Promise," she said, placing her bright yellow hard hat on her head.

Daniel went first, opening the door to let them in. It didn't appear to be structurally unsound on the inside, though Emily knew it had been deemed such. The floor was still in one piece, as was the ceiling and staircase. In fact, it looked to be in a better condition than the inn was when she had first arrived there!

Inside, the place was just an bizarre as it looked outside. There were rooms coming off rooms, a rabbit warren of corridors, and even a completely unnecessary second staircase at the back of the house leading up from the kitchen. It reminded Emily of the inn in more than one way!

She knew then that tearing it down was out of the question. It would be crime to lose all the original features, to destroy this unique piece of history. But what options did she really have? The most recent building report had deemed structurally unsound. It didn't exactly leave much wiggle room.

She thought then of the team of architects who had helped redesign Trevor's house.

"This might be a crazy idea," Emily said. "But if anyone can pull it off it's Erik & Sons."

"What idea, mommy?" Chantelle asked.

"I think we need to rebuild the house," Emily said.

Daniel frowned. "What do you mean?"

"I mean like take it apart brick by brick, salvage everything we possibly can, then put it all back together how it was before."

Roy looked surprised. "That would be very labor intensive."

"But look at it," Emily cried, throwing her arms wide. "It would be a sin not to!"

"You'd probably get in the newspapers," Daniel said. "As a local crazy woman, no doubt. But you know what they say, no publicity is bad publicity!"

She smacked him light-heartedly across the chest. "I'm being serious. What better way to honor this building than to restore it rather than demolish it? I mean it's been done before, right? With old pagan villages in the English countryside and ancient Mayan temples."

"Sure, places of historic relevance," Daniel told her. "Not just random insignificant houses in Maine."

"It's not insignificant," Emily told him. "Not to me, and not to you. Isn't that alone enough to justify it? Not to mention the fact there is nowhere like this in the whole of Maine. It will be a tourist attraction for sure. And I don't care how long it takes. It can be my labor of love."

Daniel reached out for her then and hugged her. "Emily, I've learned over the years that there is no point arguing with you. If you have a crazy dream you're going to realize it no matter what obstacles you face. So you have my backing, love. You can do this."

She squeezed him tightly, elated to finally have his support.

CHAPTER TWENTY

There was only one more day to organize everything before the New Year's Eve ball. Emily was amazed by how quickly she'd managed to pull everything together so far, but there was still so much to do.

Bryony arrived at eight a.m. for their previously postponed meeting. She bustled in through the door of the inn, her arms laden with folders, a laptop case slung over one shoulder weighing her down. As she unwrapped her huge woollen scarf from her neck, her incense scent wafted out.

"Happy Christmas, Emily," she smiled, slinging her laptop case down and dumping the folders on the reception desk. She hugged Emily. "WOW. You are so pregnant."

"I know," Emily laughed, leading the way to the kitchen where the coffee pot was brewing Bryony's fuel for the meeting. "I'm 42 weeks plus 3 days today."

"No way," Bryony said. "That's amazing. You didn't want to be induced?"

Emily tensed a little. She'd heard so many opinions about her choice she wasn't much in the mood for more criticism. "Nope," she said a little shortly.

"I think that's so brave," Bryony told her. "It can't have been easy to make that decision. Women are always being told what to do with their bodies, it takes a lot of guts to stand up and do things your own way."

Emily was surprised to get support from Bryony. Her cheeks grew warm. "Well, thank you. I just think Baby Charlotte is smart enough to pick her own birthday."

Bryony laughed. "I love that!"

Emily poured her a mug of coffee and they went back through to the guest lounge, collecting Bryony's folders on the way. They sat together in the couch that Bryony favored, placing the pile of paperwork on the coffee table before them.

"It looks like you've been working super hard," Emily said, eyeing the stack of papers.

"Yup," Bryony smiled. "With all that time on my hands with Thanksgiving and Christmas I needed something to do!"

She opened up the first folder.

"The good news is we've sold all the tickets to the ball."

Emily's eyes widened. "We have? But there were over a thousand of them!"

"I know," Bryony smiled. "Roman is a real drawer." But then her smile faded. "Now for the bad news."

"Oh…" Emily started. That wasn't what she'd been hoping to hear.

Bryony handed a piece of paper to Emily.

"These are our current room booking figures as they stand, for the inn, the carriage house, and Trevor's. As you can see our winter advertizing scheme failed."

Her heart heavy, Emily looked at the information. There were hardly any bookings for January and February. But as she looked past those months, she saw that March was over fifty percent booked up. And beyond that, the figures got dramatically better.

"Wait," Emily said as she absorbed all the information. "Is this right?"

"I know," Bryony said glumly. "I really wanted to be at least fifty percent for January and February."

"No," Emily interrupted. "That's now what I mean. The spring bookings. This says we've booked every single room in both inns?"

Bryony nodded. "Oh yeah. We're fully booked for next spring and summer. The island is as well. But if we look at the rest of winter…"

But Emily couldn't care less about the rest of winter. She was thrilled with what she was seeing. "Who cares about winter! Look at this, Bryony! I mean, this is amazing. This will provide us with more than enough income to make up for the dip this season. I can't wait to tell the staff. They were so pissed I had to lay them off over Christmas. The fact I can pay them to work at the ball is the only reason any of them are talking to me right now. But now I can pay them their missed earnings!"

She grabbed Bryony's cheeks and planted a kiss on each one.

"Oh," Bryony said, pushing her now wonky glasses back up her nose. "I thought you'd be upset about the winter scheme failing."

"I mean of course it would be better to be booked out all year round," Emily said. "But we can't expect everything to be perfect from the get go. We'll learn from our mistakes this year and approach next year differently. But for now, I think we should just celebrate the good news. Don't you?"

Bryony looked extremely relieved. "Next year, we'll make sure we have the best marketing scheme ever. I promise. My goal is a twelve month consecutive fully booked year."

"That sounds like a great goal," Emily told her.

Just then, the doorbell rang. Emily stood. "This will be the decorations for the ball." Reminding herself of the good news, she added, "Which we've sold a thousand tickets for!"

She went to the door and directed the delivers to the ballroom. When she came back through to sit with Bryony though, she saw that it was fast approaching nine a.m and the time for her doctor's appointment.

"I have to shoot," she told Bryony. "I'm having daily appointments with my doctor at the moment to make sure everything is okay with Charlotte."

Bryony gave her the thumbs up. "Good luck. I'll keep crunching the numbers."

Emily went out to the greenhouse to find Daniel. He was busy helping Chantelle plant a shrub whilst Roy watched on. It was a heartwarming scene, Emily thought, to see them all working together like that. And the greenhouse was looking superb as well.

"It's time to leave for my appointment," she said when Daniel turned and noticed her standing there.

"Are you guys okay to finish off here?" Daniel asked.

Chantelle nodded, wiping tendrils of hair from her forehead with a muddy hand, leaving streaks across it. "Good luck mommy," she said. "I think it's going to be today, you know."

"Really?" Emily said. "Well, fingers crossed."

She and Daniel headed out of the greenhouse and went through the garden to the front of the inn, before climbing into Daniel's truck.

"What do you think?" she asked him, looking over as he revved the engine. "Is Chantelle right? Will it be today?"

"I'm starting to think it will be never," Daniel replied. "That you'll be pregnant for eternity."

Emily just laughed.

They began the short, familiar journey to Doctor Arkwright's. Emily certainly wasn't going to miss this, these tense trips with Daniel, the fighting for what she felt was right. She'd be extremely happy when she didn't have to see Doctor Arkwright every single day as well. As much as she liked her, she felt silently judged each time she visited.

They reached the office at nine on the dot and were shown straight through to the doctor's room.

"How are you today?" Rose Arkwright asked. "Ready for your tests?"

"Yup," Emily said, making sure she didn't absorb anyone's judgement or negativity, staying calm in her resolve.

She knew the routine off by heart now. Blood pressure check. Visual examination. Internal examination. She'd been so daunted by it all at the beginning of her pregnancy but now she was so used to it it didn't faze her at all.

"Looks like baby's in a good position now," the doctor said, feeling Emily's bump. "Definitely downward. That's great."

Emily smiled and inched back onto the bed, bringing her legs up. Doctor Arkwright began her examination and Emily stared at the ceiling, expecting to hear the same news: no change, no sign of labor. But this time the news was different.

"And I can see signs of effacement," the doctor said. "I think it's safe to say you're in pre-labour."

"No way," Emily said, grinning from ear to ear. It felt so validating to know she'd been right to hold out for a natural birth. "Thank God."

She looked over at Daniel. He seemed relieved.

"How long are we looking at now, doctor?" he asked.

"Well pre-labor can last for a few days," she explained. "So I don't think we need to be heading to the hospital just yet."

"Days," Daniel murmured. He looked awestruck, like he really had convinced himself Emily would be pregnant for eternity.

Emily could see the twinkling of excitement and love in eyes. In a matter of days they would finally get to meet their little girl.

She sat up, grinning from ear to ear. "Thank you, doctor."

"It's been a pleasure. Honestly, good luck with the birth. I'll keep my nine a.m. appointment with you tomorrow in case there's no labor in the next twenty four hours, okay?"

They all shook hands, and Emily and Daniel left the doctor's office in high spirits.

The mood as they climbed back into the pickup truck was better than it had been for weeks. Emily felt so happy and validated in her decision. She'd known all along that her body knew what it was doing, and that her sister's spirit was watching her and guiding her through the whole thing. More than ever, she felt the spirit of Charlotte with her. She held her bump, feeling now how distinctly the baby had adjusted into position. It was happening. It was really happening. Just a little bit more patience and her dream would finally come true.

*

Back at the inn, Emily felt like her head was in the clouds. She floated around the inn, decorating the ballroom with white satin bows and gorgeous floral bouquets in preparation for tomorrow's ball. Everything was coming together so wonderfully, like there had been some grand plan in place all along.

She heard the doorbell ring and headed out of the ballroom, wondering who it might be. She answered the door to an extremely smartly dressed woman with dark hair piled into a tight bun on top of her head.

"Emily," she said, extending a hand. "I'm Jennifer Sutcliffe, an auctioneer and associate of Rico's. I wanted to speak to you about the collection of William Gamble kitchenware you've recently come into possession of."

"Oh wonderful," Emily said. "Please come in."

She led Jennifer into the lounge, seating her at the round table in the bay windows.

"What a gorgeous house," Jennifer said.

"Thanks," Emily smiled. "We're an inn, actually. It's a bit chaotic here as we're preparing for a ball tomorrow."

"Not the one with Roman Westbrook playing at?" she asked.

"Yes," Emily laughed. "You've heard about it?"

"I'm coming," Jennifer replied, laughing. "My sister and I are huge fans. Both recently divorced. Felt like we deserved a great night out. How funny. I had no idea this place was here. I'd heard of a new inn opening up nearby but thought it was in that old Queen Anne building on the sea front."

"You don't come to town meetings, clearly," Emily said, chuckling. "That inn was rejected. But funnily enough, I'm using the money from the sale of the silver to buy the building. I want to rescue it from disrepair. It's so unique and beautiful."

"How fantastic," Jennifer replied.

Pleasantries aside, it was time to get down to business.

"So Rico explained that I have some William Gamble kitchen silver to sell. Would you like to see the pieces?" Emily asked.

"I'd love to," Jennifer said, grinning. She looked very excited about it. "I'm such a geek for silver kitchen ware, and I love Gamble. He was one of the Silversmiths of Soho. His son carried on the trade. Such wonderful history." She looked dreamy-eyed then before her gaze snapped back to Emily. "Sorry, I'm already going into a daydream."

Emily laughed as she stood. "No need to daydream, you can see it for yourself."

She led Jennifer along the corridor towards her study, where the silver was currently being stored behind a locked door. Emily rummaged in her pocket for the key, then twisted it in the lock and opened up the door.

There was so much silver inside, it had started to take over the entire room! Every shelf had some kind of ornate piece upon it, and her desk was covered in the smaller pieces, like the cutlery and dishes.

"Here it is," Emily said.

She turned to face Jennifer and saw that the woman's mouth was hanging open in surprise. A hand fluttered to her chest.

"Incredible," she murmured.

She paced inside, looking lost as if she didn't know where to go first, then finally headed towards a coffee pot standing on top of the filing cabinet. She took it down, turning it delicately in her hands to look at its underside.

"There is it," she gasped, letting out a little squeal. "William Gamble's official silversmith's stamp." She looked over her shoulder at Emily. "It was law, you see, to have this unique stamp. Every sivlersmith had to make a stamp on a lead plate that was sorted in Goldsmith's Hall, which consisted of the silversmith's initials. It was a way of both guaranteeing the standard of silver, and also helping identify cases of fraud, because no matter how closely someone may try to copy the mark, fraudulent copies would never perfectly match the leaden plate." She turned back in wonder at the coffee pot. "I love that feeling of holding a piece of history."

"So it's definitely genuine then?" Emily asked.

"Oh yes," Jennifer gushed. She put the pot down and picked up a dish beside it, nodding when her gaze found Gamble's mark. "Yes, yes. Of course, I'll need to authenticate each one before I can say conclusively. It may take a while."

"Please, take as long as you need. Shall I bring some tea? Coffee?"

Jennifer shook her head. "No, thank you. I'll be quite fine."

She sat down and began making a list, checking each piece's authenticity. Emily watched her, curious about the process, and amused by the way Jennifer behaved like a kid in a candy store with each new piece Emily handed her.

When the list was complete, Jennifer confirmed they were all, indeed, authentic pieces.

"Fifty-two items," she told Emily. "How marvellous."

"What happens next?" Emily asked.

"Well, you'll be pleased to know that I already have a potential buyer in England. They're ancestors of William Gamble, and his son Ellis who continued his work after him. They're very keen to snap up pieces as and when they becomes available. I'd hazard a guess that they would pay a very handsome price just to avoid the risk of losing them at auction."

"Really?" Emily asked, surprised.

Jennifer nodded. "Of course, as an auctioneer I'd always recommend auctioning them. A collection as extensive as this could fetch up to three times the amount of their worth on the day but there's always a risk involved of the sale falling through for whatever reason."

"So I have options," Emily said. "Sell immediately to the family, or hold out for auction and see if I can get a higher price."

"Precisely," Jennifer explained. "Here, this is some information on the auction process." She handed Emily some brochures. "There's lots of information in here that will help you make your decision."

"How long would each option take?" Emily asked as she took the brochures and rested them on her lap for future reading. "The auction versus selling straight to the collectors."

"Auctioning would be at least a month," Jennifer explained. "We need time to get the word out to interested parties, you see. With the collectors, I'd have to call them first to confirm, but I've worked with them in the past and it was honestly a matter of days from authentication to sale. It's sentimental for them, rather than an investment, you see."

Emily thought of Terry, of the share of the money she'd promised him. The quicker they sold the silver the quicker he'd have enough money to buy a new farm and home.

"It would also save on the hassle of getting them insured in the meantime," Jennifer explained.

"I'd not even thought of that," Emily confessed, but the lock and key approach, she realized now, was hardly the most secure way of storing expensive antiques. "You've given me a lot to think about," Emily added. "I'll speak to my family first and let you know my decision tomorrow at the ball."

"Fantastic," Jennifer said, smiling widely. "I look forward to hearing your decision tomorrow!"

Emily showed Jennifer to the door, waving her off. As Jennifer's car went down the drive, Emily saw Amy's turning in at the top of the road. She watched as she drove a little too fast towards the house, before parking diagonally and throwing open her door.

"Emily! Emily! Guess what!" she cried before she'd even fully got out of the car.

"What?" Emily exclaimed.

"The house!" Amy shouted. She hurried for the bottom step of the porch. "Our offer was accepted! We're buying the house!"

She hurried up the steps and, on reaching the top, threw herself into Emily's waiting arms.

"Oh my God, that's such great news," Emily cried, hugging her tightly. "I'm so happy for you."

"We're going to be neighbors," Amy laughed. "With nothing but some trees between us."

"Well, as long as we don't let Raven Kingsley get between us again," Emily said, her cheeks warming.

"Never," Amy replied. "That reminds me, what happened after the meeting? You went off with her because she was crying. What sob story did she give you?"

Emily chewed her lip. "Actually, well, I sort of bought the inn off her."

Amy froze, her mouth literally dropping open. "Did you really?"

Emily's bush deepened. She crinkled her nose. "Yeah. Raven wants to leave Sunset Harbor. I realized she'd never find a buyer and it just seemed to make sense at the time."

Amy still looked stunned. But not angry, Emily noted, just surprised.

"You have got to stop dropping these bombshells on me," Amy said, laughing. "Oh my God, Em, you bought a house too! We just need Daniel's shop offer to be accepted now. And your baby to be born, of course."

Emily grinned then. "You know, I have a suspicion that it's going to happen sooner rather than later. The stars are aligning, Ames. I can feel it. Everything is going to work out in the end."

*

That evening, everyone was sat around relaxing in the living room. Chantelle and Roy were putting the finishing touches onto her clock.

"There," she announced. "It's done!"

She sat back, and held the clock up to everyone.

"That's really amazing," Emily told her.

Daniel looked beyond proud. "I can't believe my little girl made that."

"Pretty much on her own as well," Roy added. "I only helped her with a few technical bits."

Chantelle grinned, clearly feeling very accomplished.

Just then, Daniel's cell phone began to ring.

"It's the agent from the shop," he said, looking shocked.

"Answer it," Emily told him, feeling excited.

Daniel did. Everyone watched with bated breath. Daniel was nodding, frowning, nodding again. Then his eyes widened. He looked up at Emily.

"Wonderful. Great. Thanks. Yes, Happy New Year to you as well." He ended the call and looked at them stunned. "My offer was accepted. The shop is mine."

Everyone erupted into cheers. Before they'd even had time to calm down, the doorbell rang.

"I can't take any more news," Emily said.

But she headed to the door, her family in tow, everyone filled with anticipation for who their mystery visitor could be. Emily opened the door and her eyes widened with shock.

Standing on her doorstep was her mother.

"Nana Patty!" Chantelle screamed.

"Mom," Emily gasped.

But Patricia's eyes were looking past her, focusing on Roy.

"Hello darling," Roy said, opening his arms for his ex wife.

Emily watched, stunned, as Patricia hurried into the inn and flew into his embrace. It had been over thirty years since they'd exchanged more than passing insults at one another, and here they were, together, burying decades of hatred and fighting.

Emily felt tears well in her eyes. Her whole family was here, united, together.

Just then, she felt a sudden tightening sensation in her back as her muscles spasmed. A pre-labor contraction. A sign from Charlotte. She realized, grinning, what Baby Charlotte had been waiting for all along. She'd been waiting for everyone to be together.

CHAPTER TWENTY ONE

"Look at you guys," Emily exclaimed, as Marnie, Lois, Vanessa, Parker, Alec and Matthew emerged into the living room in their formal attire.

Each of them was working at the ball tonight, and it felt so wonderful for Emily to have them all reunited again. The inn had felt so empty without her staff around. They looked stunning, with the boys dressed up in black tie and the girls in white satin ball gowns.

"I have some exciting news," Emily told them all. "The inn is fully booked from next April onwards. So I'm going to be able to recuperate you your lost earnings this month. I'm really sorry for the stress it must have caused you guys not knowing what was going on."

She handed them each a silver envelope. Inside each was a paycheck covering their December earnings, plus a small belated Christmas bonus. They took them gratefully, uttering their gratitude.

Emily checked the clock then. It was almost party time. The bash was beginning at eight, with Roman scheduled on stage for an hour between nine and ten, and the fireworks display starting at midnight exactly. Emily was so excited for everyone to arrive and see how incredible the ballroom looked. And she was equally excited to know both her parents were going to be in attendance.

Everyone left the living room. Marnie and Lois took their positions at the main entrance to the inn, whilst the others headed towards the ballroom. Emily dimmed the main foyer lights, turning on the twinkling little fairy light trail that led the way to the ballroom. It looked great. Then she turned on the music -- a collection of classy classical pieces -- and hurried off to the ballroom to make sure everything was perfect.

Inside, the ballroom looked stunning. Blue lights made the whole place look like a winter palace. There was an ice sculpture in the center of the room, shaped like a frozen fountain. Around the perimeter of the ballroom there were chairs and bistro tables, each one adorned with flowers and an ice bucket for orders of champagne. Raj Patel had come early to fuss over the floral displays, making sure each one was perfect.

Across the other side of the ballroom was the stage, which had a backdrop of black velvet and twinkling lights to look like a midnight sky. Owen was making his way around the instruments to check they were all in tune, and Serena watched on. They were using the evening as their unofficial leaving party, because they'd be leaving for Singapore in just a few days time.

Emily noticed that sitting to one side were all her nearest and dearest; Roy, Patricia, Daniel, Chantelle and Terry. They all looked fabulous in their glitzy party clothes. Even the dogs were sporting big bows on their collars. She made a beeline for her family, her heart swelling with love for them as she approached.

Daniel reached for her when she got there and kissed her hand. "Are the staff all caught up?"

"Yes, they were thrilled by the news," she told him. "I'm so glad to have been able to offer them their old shifts back."

"We have a lot to thank Brynony for," Daniel added. "She's been a real star."

"She has."

Emily's sentence was cut off by another twinge in her back. Her pre-labour contractions were completely sporadic, sometimes lasting for a long time, sometimes only fleeting. There was no rhythm to them, which was the only way she knew she wasn't properly in labour yet. But everyone reminded her that Baby Charlotte was getting ready to make her appearance. 42+4, Doctor Arkwright had confirmed with a whistle in their appointment that morning, followed by, "I've never known anyone go this long!"

Emily touched her stomach then, the velvet fabric of her dress stretched taught against it. Charlotte had been waiting for her family to surround her and now they were. They just needed to employ a little more patience, that was all.

Just then, the first guests began to arrive, filtering in through the large white lace curtain hanging over the ballroom entrance. They were strangers to Emily, but she could tell from their expressions that they were delighted by what they saw. It felt like a new step to have people come to one of her parties who she didn't already know. They'd chosen to purchase a ticket and spend a special evening in her establishment. She wanted to make sure everyone had the best time ever.

More and more people began to enter, some familiar Sunset Harbor folk and an equal amount of strangers from out of town. Then Emily noticed Jennifer Sutcliffe arriving with her sister.

"That's her," she said, grabbing Daniel's arm. "That's the auctioneer for the silver. I told her I'd let her know our decision about the English collectors. What do you think we should do? Hold on and take the risk for a higher payout, or sell it now and have the security of the income?"

Daniel took her by the shoulders and turned her in the direction of Terry. He was chatting animatedly to Patricia, both of them holding champagne flutes and taking sips between laughter.

"I think we should sell for him," Daniel told her. "So his life doesn't have to be on pause anymore. I think he deserves it."

Emily nodded. "I think so too."

She kissed Daniel, grateful for the support and compassion he had shown. Then she disengaged from his embrace and approached Jennifer and her sister.

"Emily, hi," Jennifer said, putting the vol a vant she'd been halfway through eating into a napkin. "This is my sister Clarissa. Clar, this is the woman I was telling you about, with the William Gamble collection."

"You're one lucky lady," Clarissa said. "You're taking up Jennifer's offer aren't you, to sell straight to the English collectors?"

"That's what I'm here to talk about," Emily said with a decisive nod. "I'd like to go ahead with the sale."

"Fantastic!" Jennifer cried. Forgetting any sense of formality, she threw her arms around Emily, making bits of pastry fly from her wrapped vol a vont into the air.

Emily laughed.

"I'm going to call them straight away," Jennifer said then, taking her cell phone from her purse. Then she paused. "Wait, what time is Roman Westbrook on stage?"

"You've got a little while yet," Emily told her, giggling.

Jennifer hurried off to make her call.

The moment she'd left, Serena came up to Emily.

"This is amazing," she gushed. Emily noticed tears twinkling in her eyes. "I'm going to miss you so much when I leave."

"Me too," Emily told her. "Remember none of this success would have been possible without you. You were my first real friend in Sunset Harbor. I'll never forget all the help you gave me at the beginning, getting the inn off the ground."

Serena began to cry then in earnest. "I just wish I could have been more available over the last year. I let life get in the way, my degree, Owen, all that stuff."

"You put your happiness first," Emily said. "I'd never resent you that."

Serena wiped her tears away. "Can I tell you a secret?"

"Of course," Emily said, taking her hands.

"We're going to get married. Owen and I. Once we're settled in Singapore."

"Well that's fantastic news!" Emily gushed, hugging her tightly. "You're the sweetest couple in the world. I'm so happy for you."

"Thank you," Serena blushed. "You get to know first because I want you to be one of my bridesmaids."

"I'd love to," Emily told her. Returning the favor Serena had given her would be an honor. "Of course I would."

Serena let out an exhalation. "Thank you. You have no idea how long I've been wanting to tell someone that!"

Emily chuckled, and Serena seemed to relax considerably, returning to her usual chatty, confident demeanor.

"So when is this baby coming?" she asked. "If I don't meet her before I leave I'll be devastated."

"I'm in pre-labor right now," Emily explained. "Which is why I keep wincing in pain and grabbing my lower back!"

Serena's eyes widened. "No way. Now? Does that mean she'll come any minute?"

"They're not proper contractions. Not yet. But it's definitely getting closer!"

"Are you scared?" Serena asked.

Emily shook her head. "I'm excited. I have my whole family around me for the first time in decades. And if Charlotte has it her way, I'll have the whole of the town around me too! I couldn't have asked for better timing to be honest with you."

Jennifer returned then, her face a huge grin.

"Emily," she said, "I'm going to give you a piece of paper and the figure on it is the amount that you're going to receive for the sale of the silver collection. You may want to sit down."

Emily took the slip of paper and read the numbers written upon it in cursive writing.

Four hundred and fifty three thousand dollars

Emily's mouth became extremely dry. She fanned her face. It was four times the amount she'd been expecting.

"I have to tell Terry," she managed to say.

She staggered across the dance floor.

"Excuse me, Terry," she said, pulling his arm towards her and away from Patricia. She spoke in a hushed voice. "I have some news. About the silver."

Terry moved away, shaking his head. "I told you, I can't accept that money. And besides, I've found a new place to live, with space for a Christmas tree farm. Once the insurance payment comes through I'll be back on my feet."

"Terry, you have to allow me to help you," Emily said. "At least as an investor in your business."

He paused then, tilting his head to the side. "As an investor? Well that would certainly be more palatable to me."

"Good," Emily said. "We'll sort out the fine details later. But just know I'm looking to invest no less than two hundred thousand dollars in your business."

Terry's mouth dropped open with shock. "That would be one hell of a Christmas tree farm."

Patricia came over then.

"What are you talking about?" she demanded. "You both look like you're about to pass out."

"Just some good business news," Emily told her. "We're planning on working together in the future, aren't we Terry?"

Terry still looked stunned. He reached for Emily, hugging her tightly. "How can I ever repay your kindness?"

"You could start by dancing with my mother," Emily chuckled into his ear. "She seems quite taken with you."

"Consider it done!" Terry laughed, and he turned to Patricia, offering his hand. "A dance, my lady?"

She looked horrified. "Me? Dance?"

But Terry wasn't going to take no for an answer. He grasped her hand and pulled her to the dance floor. Patricia didn't even try to hide her delighted smile as she allowed him to twirl her around.

Emily watched on as more and more of her friends arrived; Yvonne with Keiran, Wesley and Suzanna, Cynthia, Karen, Mayor Hansen. They were all dressed to the nines, and all here to see in the New Year with her. She felt overwhelmed with love and gratitude for this little town. Then she saw Roy and Chantelle dancing together, the girl standing on his feet just as Emily had done at her age. A lump formed in her throat. Tomorrow Roy would be leaving, but tonight they would celebrate and enjoy every last second of the time they had together.

CHAPTER TWENTY TWO

Fireworks ushered in the new year and soon, night rolled into day. Each room at the inn began to fill up with tired residents who didn't want the celebrations to end just yet. To Emily surprise, she soon had a fully booked inn!

She left the ball in the capable hands of her staff and went to get some much needed rest. But at six a.m. she woke suddenly to the sensation of a strong contraction. Her first proper one. Labor had begun.

She turned and shook Daniel awake.

"I just had a contraction," she told him. "A proper one."

Daniel's eyes widened with excitement and fear. "Really? It's going to be today? We're going to meet our daughter today?"

"We have to start timing them," Emily told him.

He scrabbled for his cell phone on the bedside table. "Okay. The stopwatch is running. How do you feel?"

"I'm excited," Emily told him. "I can't wait. We ought to wake up Chantelle though, and mom and dad."

Daniel tore back the covers. "Okay. Yes. I'll do that right now."

He pulled Emily's bathrobe on, and Emily couldn't help but giggle at the panicked sight of him. He hurried out, calling Chantelle's name loudly. Clearly he'd quite forgotten that their inn was fully booked. Emily heard the sound of doors opening and people exclaiming with delight that her labor had started. She blushed as she listened to the call go up, spreading through the entire inn. And considering most of the town folk had stayed overnight at the inn that meant the entire town now knew!

She got out of bed gently, touching her stomach with awe, knowing it would soon be gone. She wondered if the strange sense of grief she felt was normal. She'd become so used to have Charlotte as a part of her, she would miss her when she was on the outside, so to speak!

The door flew open and in ran Chantelle.

"Is she coming? Is it happening?"

Emily ruffled her hair. "I was just woken by my first contraction. It'll take a little while though, so don't get too excited! We'll have plenty of time for breakfast."

Chantelle pouted. "Okay. Can we have pancakes?"

"Definitely," Emily said.

They went downstairs, still in their night clothes. To Emily's surprise and delight, many of the guests had now gotten up, roused by the alarm, and were in the dining room waiting for her. Either that, or an early breakfast shift to begin.

As she entered, they erupted into applause. Friends came up to her, kissing her cheeks, wishing her the best.

"Thanks," Emily blushed. She felt another sudden contraction and stopped dead in her tracks. "Oh boy, that seriously is not pleasant."

Two people stood suddenly and rushed forward -- Sunita Patel and Rose Arkwright. They both offered Emily a seat, laughing as they bumped shoulders.

Emily took the seat and smiled up at the two doctors. "I didn't know you were at the ball," she said to Doctor Arkwright. "It was so busy I didn't manage to greet everyone."

"I wasn't going to miss a Roman Westbrook gig," the doctor replied. "No chance!"

Daniel came into the dining room then, taking in the sight of Emily huddled in the chair in the clear grips of a contraction.

"Okay, that was six minutes," he told her. He looked appealing at the two doctors. "How are we doing?"

"You're fine for now," Rose replied. "You can have some breakfast. Take it easy. I'll take over the timing."

The door opened then and in came Terry, Matthew and Parker, carrying trays of pancakes. Emily couldn't help but find the whole thing amusing -- in between the bursts excruciating pain, that was. Usually she hated being the center of attention but right now she didn't mind at all. In fact, it was extremely comforting having everyone around her.

"Where's my dad?" Emily asked, searching the crowd and finding Amy.

"He must still be sleeping," she said. "It's super early after all."

Emily shook her head. "He always wakes up early." She felt a surge of panic. "Can someone go and search for him?"

Several people leapt up, including Chantelle and Amy, and went off to search the inn for Roy.

"Is that him?" someone said.

Emily looked up and saw they were pointing out the large windows. Out on the grass, Roy was pacing backwards and forwards, looking like he was lost in thought. A sense of relief overcame Emily to see he was alive and well, even though his pacing behavior troubled her.

Through the window, she saw Chantelle run up to him, tugging him by the elbow. They exchanged some words, then a huge hug. Chantelle pointed back at the inn, next, and Roy's expression changed. He took her hand and they trudged back together.

Emily looked up to the door, waiting for them to emerge through. Roy was first.

"You're in labor?" he asked, sounding concerned but excited at the same time.

Emily nodded. "The contractions have just started. We have time for breakfast though. Please, take a seat."

Roy sat opposite her, accepting a plate of pancakes from Matthew.

"What was that conversation about with Chantelle?" she asked Roy as she attempted to eat through the echoes of pain.

"She asked me if I was leaving today," Roy said. "And I told her that I didn't want to. I don't want to go home, Emily. I want to stay with you. To see out my last fews weeks here, with my family, in this place I love."

Emily hiccuped her emotion. "Dad, I want that more than anything," she said.

"Really?" he asked. "I could live here with you until.. Until I pass?"

She nodded, feeling tears of relief spring from her eyes. "Yes! I can take care of you here."

"Even with a newborn?"

"Even with a newborn."

Just then, another huge contraction took hold of her. Rose Arkwright leapt up from her seat.

"They're getting quicker, and fast. Emily, I think it's time."

The whole room erupted into a hubbub of noise. Emily grit her teeth and looked around at her friends eager expressions, at Daniel's look of awe, terror and excitement. She waited until the pain subsided and allowed Daniel and Roy to help her to her feet.

"I should probably say goodbye in that case," Emily said to the room. She paused, glancing around again at all the faces of everyone she loved. "You'll come and visit, won't you? At the hospital? I'd hate to be there alone again."

She was met with a huge chorus of "YES!" and people telling her to "GO!"

Laughing, Emily turned, taking Daniel's arm.

"Ready to meet our little girl?" she asked him.

"I've never been more ready," he told her, smiling back.

Together, they headed for the door. Emily didn't feel scared at all. All she felt was the warmth and love behind her, coming from her inn and all the people inside whom she adored. This was what Charlotte had been waiting for all along. This was the perfect moment for her to enter the world; a new year, a new beginning, surrounded by an abundance of love.

NOW AVAILABLE!

LOVE LIKE THIS
(The Romance Chronicles—Book #1)

"Sophie Love's ability to impart magic to her readers is exquisitely wrought in powerfully evocative phrases and descriptions....[This is] the perfect romance or beach read, with a difference: its enthusiasm and beautiful descriptions offer an unexpected attention to the complexity of not just evolving love, but evolving psyches. It's a delightful recommendation for romance readers looking for a touch more complexity from their romance reads."
--*Midwest Book Review* (Diane Donovan re: *For Now and Forever*)

"A very well written novel, describing the struggle of a woman to find her true identity. The author did an amazing job with the creation of the characters and her description of the environment. The romance is there, but not overdosed. Kudos to the author for this amazing start of a series that promises to be very entertaining."
--*Books and Movies Reviews*, Roberto Mattos (re: *For Now and Forever*)

LOVE LIKE THIS (The Romance Chronicles—Book #1) is the debut of a new romance series by #1 bestselling author Sophie Love.

Keira Swanson, 28, lands her dream job at *Viatorum*, a slick magazine in New York City, as an aspiring travel writer. But their culture is brutal, her boss is a monster, and she doesn't know if she can last for long.

That changes when Keira, by a fluke, is handed a coveted assignment and given her big chance: to travel to Ireland for 30 days, witness the legendary Lisdoonvarna festival of love, and to debunk the myth that true love exists. Keira, cynical herself and in a rocky place with her long-term boyfriend, is all too happy to oblige.

But when Keira falls in love with Ireland and meets her Irish tour guide, who just may be the man of her dreams, she is no longer sure of anything.

A whirlwind romantic comedy that is as profound as it is funny, LOVE LIKE THIS is book #1 in the debut of a dazzling new romance series that will make you laugh, cry, and will keep you turning pages late into the night—and will make you fall in love with romance all over again.

Book #2 in The Romance Chronicles is now also available!

Sophie Love

#1 bestselling author Sophie Love is author of the romantic comedy series THE INN AT SUNSET HARBOR, which includes eight books, and which begins with FOR NOW AND FOREVER (THE INN AT SUNSET HARBOR—BOOK 1).

Sophie Love is also the author of the debut romantic comedy series, THE ROMANCE CHRONICLES, which begins with LOVE LIKE THIS (THE ROMANCE CHRONICLES—BOOK 1).

Sophie would love to hear from you, so please visit www.sophieloveauthor.com to email her, to join the mailing list, to receive free ebooks, to hear the latest news, and to stay in touch!

BOOKS BY SOPHIE LOVE

THE INN AT SUNSET HARBOR
FOR NOW AND FOREVER (Book #1)
FOREVER AND FOR ALWAYS (Book #2)
FOREVER, WITH YOU (Book #3)
IF ONLY FOREVER (Book #4)
FOREVER AND A DAY (Book #5)
FOREVER, PLUS ONE (Book #6)
FOR YOU, FOREVER (Book #7)
CHRISTMAS FOREVER (Book #8)

THE ROMANCE CHRONICLES
LOVE LIKE THIS (Book #1)
LOVE LIKE THAT (Book #2)
LOVE LIKE OURS (Book #3)
LOVE LIKE THEIRS (Book #4)

Made in the USA
Lexington, KY
08 September 2018